DO NOT REMOVE
CARDS FROM POCKET

LARGE PRINT

NUTS IN MAY

When Teddy's father, a busy publisher, leaves for the U.S.A., who should arrive but Teddy's uncle, Lord Brickwood, absent these many years in Hong Kong and, it begins to dawn on Teddy, the black goat of the family? Lord Brickwood has a very shaky memory about which London clubs he belongs to, and he's not too reliable about mundane things like bank accounts, old girl-friends and exactly what he did in the War. Teddy soon finds he has his hands full with Uncle, and his flat full of the most extraordinary people coming and going. Richard Gordon is on top form and proves yet again that he is one of the leading English humorists.

NUTS IN MAY

Richard Gordon

A Lythway Book

CHIVERS PRESS
BATH

First published 1964
by
William Heinemann Ltd
This Large Print edition published by
Chivers Press
by arrangement with William Heinemann Ltd
and in the U.S.A. with Curtis Brown Group Ltd
1983

ISBN 0 85046 940 6

© Richard Gordon Ltd, 1964

British Library Cataloguing in Publication Data

Gordon, Richard, *1921–*
    Nuts in May.—Large print ed.—
    (A Lythway book)
    Rn: Gordon Ostlere   I. Title
    823'.914 (F]   PR6057.014

    ISBN 0–85046–940–6

To Lucy

NUTS IN MAY

CHAPTER ONE

'My dear boy, what on earth's the matter with you?' asked Mr. Algernon Brickwood, the well-known publisher who furthered the cause of English Literature a good deal over luncheon in the best restaurants. 'Here we are in the spring, when a young man's fiancée lightly turns to thoughts of love—how is dear Abigail, by the way?'

His son Teddy glanced up from studying the pattern on the tablecloth. 'Abigail? Oh, Abigail. She's fine, Father. Absolutely fine.'

'I'm delighted to hear it. And there you sit, looking as though you'd just found the moth in your sackcloth and ashes. Sometimes I can't understand you younger generation at all.'

'I'm just a bit out of condition, I suppose,' Teddy countered quickly, fiddling with one of those comic sticks of Italian bread. 'My sinuses seem due for a decoke and rebore. Not getting enough exercise. And overwork, of course,' he added.

But Mr. Brickwood was deep in the menu murmuring, 'Ah asparagus.' Publishing is a strenuous trade leaving a man with an appetite for his lunch, as the head waiters of all the best restaurants could tell you.

'Father—' Teddy burst out suddenly.

1

He was interrupted by the waiter shoving a dish of preliminary olives in front of him, shooting the young man a cagey glance. The way Teddy had been twitching and making little bunnies out of his napkin was attracting attention.

'Father—' Teddy repeated, nervously snapping the bread in two.

Fact is, the poor fellow was about to unveil the blot on the family escutcheon, and wondering whether to do it with the asparagus or risk his parent choking over something more solid.

'Such a delightful surprise finding you in Town for the day from Oxford,' his old man prattled on, taking no notice. 'How on earth did you wangle an exeat so early in the term? The dentist, I suppose? When I was up myself it was always considered essential to have one's teeth attended within easy reach of the West End. What anniversary is it?'

Teddy looked puzzled. 'Anniversary?'

'Yes, you've been perched in the tree of knowledge long enough to have such things at your fingertips. Surely in our long and glorious history *something* must have happened today?'

'I rather think it was the Battle of Tewkesbury in 1471,' Teddy supplied obligingly.

'Excellent! Let us toast the illustrious memory of the Battle of Tewkesbury. My doctor,' Mr. Brickwood explained, 'allows me to drink only an occasional glass in celebration of some special occasion. Waiter!'

He ordered a bottle of champagne.

When you've screwed yourself up to make the most shattering revelation of your life and get sidetracked into the Battle of Tewkesbury, it's difficult to set the release mechanism again. Mr. Brickwood tucked into his lunch happily enough, jumping up between mouthfuls of roast duck to kiss passing actresses. He was a little fat chap with ginger tweed suits, gold-rimmed glasses, a Lloyd George haircut, and a Hannen Swaffer tie, the sort of publisher disappearing from the London literary scene like authors' beards and the horsewhipping of editors, and to my mind leaving it the poorer. But Teddy sat picking at his plate, deaf to the gay sounds of expensive nourishment all round, looking like a nervous saboteur with the time bomb in his suitcase who's suddenly discovered his wristwatch had stopped.

It wasn't until they'd reached the delicious imported strawberries with the nauseating price that he squared his shoulders and announced abruptly, 'I should like to talk about my future.'

'Your future?' Into Mr. Brickwood's eye came that soft glance of proud and affectionate possession, as though inspecting the option clause in a best-selling author's contract. 'But my dear boy, your future is so shining bright it

3

might have been scrubbed down with one of those ghastly detergents you keep seeing on the telly.'

'Quite, Father, but—'

'This summer you will take your degree, which is more than I did for a start,' the publisher outlined fondly. 'Then on July the thirtieth you will be joined in matrimony with Abigail Fitzhammond, at what the newspapers will undoubtedly describe as the wedding of the year. I know that I for one shall enjoy it immensely.'

'Exactly, Father, though—'

'Brushing off the bridesmaids and confetti, you will leave for a blissful honeymoon at her father's charming villa in Spain.' He scooped up the remains of his strawberries as neatly as the subsidiary rights of a novel. 'Before returning to live happily ever after in the delightful house her father has so thoughtfully placed at your disposal in Knightsbridge. Any more anniversaries?'

'Well, yesterday was Machiavelli's birthday.'

'Splendid! I charge my glass to wish his shade many happy returns. I do wish you'd cheer up a bit, Teddy,' his old man broke off testily. 'You needn't sit there fidgeting like a little girl in a new woolly vest. There's loads of time to catch the afternoon train back to Oxford.'

Teddy gave a gulp. 'I'm not going back to Oxford.'

4

'Oh, really? Got fed up with the place?'

'The other way round, I'm afraid.'

'What, sent down?'

Teddy nodded.

'By George! What for? Women, drink, cards, or climbing?'

Teddy took a bite at the corner of his napkin. 'Nothing like that,' he answered dully. 'Those sort of larks don't go on much at Oxford these days, anyway.' He shifted a bit in his chair. 'Of course, Father, you've heard of *The Abattoir*?'

'Never in my life.'

'It's a little undergraduate review I put on with George Churchyard in College.'

The sad story was poured out with the coffee.

Teddy Brickwood was a bright lad with all the youthful charm of a freshly boiled new potato, but he had a weakness for doing imitations of the lot they used to call Our Elders and Betters but now go by name of The Establishment. It was always getting him into trouble at school, particularly his rather diverting impression of the afternoon the headmaster swallowed a wasp. So you see how neatly he was born into his times. Ever since *Beyond the Fringe* little satirical shows have been opening all over the place, as acid as a load of unripe grapefruit. Clever young men right and left are doing brilliant imitations of the Prime Minister, the Archbishop of Canterbury, Mao Tse-tung, and so on, and generally taking the sacred cow by

5

the horns. At Oxford, Teddy and George Churchyard were soon being pointed out in the Broad and whispered about in the recesses of the Bodleian. They got their photographs in the *Isis* and their rooms ragged by the rugger fifteen. They seemed set for one of those terrific Oxford reputations, just like Cardinal Newman.

But unfortunately the star turn of *The Abattoir* was their take-off of Professor Needler.

If you manage to keep awake on Sunday afternoons you'll have seen Professor Needler and his telly show *I Know the Answer*. He's one of those new type Oxford dons. No longer are they amiable old birds pottering round the dreaming spires in moth-eaten gowns, awash with port and wondering where they left their bicycles. These days they're all crew cut and library glasses with a sharp eye for a camera angle and their agents doing them over their percentage. The Prime Minister, the Archbishop of Canterbury and Mao Tse-tung could take it. But not Professor Needler.

'I thought I told you gentlemen on two separate occasions to remove that scurrilous item from your juvenile performance?' he had addressed the pair of satirists in his rooms.

'I'm terribly sorry, sir,' Teddy apologized nervously. 'But the audience were laughing so much I suppose we got carried away.'

'And so you shall be,' returned the Professor neatly. 'I have had a word with the Master and

6

you will both kindly see you are out of College by tomorrow night.'

'I suppose he thought it might interfere with his TAM rating,' Teddy ended miserably over the lunch table, sitting back and eyeing his father with the expression of the Prodigal Son having just rung the doorbell.

There was a brief silence among the surrounding clatter of cutlery.

'My boy—' Mr. Brickwood's voice quivered with emotion. 'My boy, I am proud of you.'

'Proud?' Teddy glanced up.

'Yes, proud,' repeated Mr. Brickwood. 'To be sent down from Oxford shows a refreshing independence of mind in an otherwise hopelessly hidebound institution. To be chucked out for protesting against that self-opinionated overblown schoolmaster—that pedlar of predigested intellectual babyfood—who moreover totally ruins all my Sundays, that's sheer martyrdom!'

Teddy's face took on the look of the man against the wall bravely refusing the eye-bandage and last cigarette, noticing a bloke on a horse galloping over the horizon waving a bit of paper explaining the verdict was all a ghastly mistake.

'That's absolutely wonderful of you, Father.' For the first time he raised a smile. 'I mean, taking it like that.'

'I may be somewhat old-fashioned in my

views,' explained Mr. Brickwood solemnly, 'but I believe it is a parent's duty always to back up his son. If a young man cannot expect sympathy from his own father'—he dabbed briefly behind the gold rims with his handkerchief—'the world is indeed a sorry, sorry place.'

'I'm afraid it rather knocks the Foreign Office on the head, though,' Teddy admitted.

He had been earmarked for the diplomatic lark, and widely expected to be going round in no time at all wearing knee breeches and doing the dirty on foreign prime ministers.

'That is of little consequence,' conceded Mr. Brickwood loftily. 'I wouldn't ask you to join the family firm, my boy. Once there was no more pleasant nor instructive way for a young man just down from Oxford to lose three or four thousand pounds than in publishing, but with all these paperbacks it's no longer an occupation for gentlemen. I'm sure Abigail's father will have no difficulty fitting you somewhere into his enormous organization.'

'Oh, there's just one thing.' Teddy gave a little laugh. 'Abigail and I have broken it off.'

'What!' Mr. Brickwood knocked his champagne glass flying, startling the party enjoying *crêpes Suzettes* at the next table. 'Broken it off? Broken what off? Broken your engagement off?'

Teddy nodded. 'Yes, I suppose we'll have to put a line in *The Times* informing the public the fixture's been scratched. But I can easily do that this afternoon.' He gave a wry grin. 'After all, now I've nothing much else on my hands.'

'Ye gods!' Mr. Brickwood thumped the table, squashing a rather nasty *petit four*. 'How in the hell did this happen?'

Teddy looked surprised. 'It was about the fish.'

'The fish?'

He nodded. 'I'll explain.' He noticed his parent had turned all purple and shaky, like the port jelly being dished out at the table opposite. 'By the way,' he added quickly. 'I've just remembered—today was the Battle of Seringapatam, 1799.'

CHAPTER TWO

It's an odd thing, but if you bury your head in the sands long enough, when Fate starts tweaking out your tail-feathers it's soon grabbing them by the handful.

Only a couple of days before his interview with Professor Needler, Teddy Brickwood was one of the happiest young men ever to run up a bill at Blackwell's or down a pint in the Randolph. It was one of those glorious May afternoons, with Oxford warming its old stones in the spring sunshine, and as he gazed from the mullioned windows of his rooms the only movement in the silent quad was the flowers stirring sleepily in their window-boxes. Behind him, tea was already laid on the table, with cucumber sandwiches. The kettle purred contentedly on the gas ring. At his side on the window-seat nestled one of the most beautiful girls in London.

'Charming weather,' Teddy observed.

'Yes, darling,' she said.

He gave a sigh. 'Only another three months,' he went on, 'before you and I will be standing among all the cut glass and silverware handing round cake as man and wife.'

'Yes, darling,' she said.

'Hardly believable sometimes, is it?'

'Yes, darling,' she said.

He paused while the Oxford clocks, a body of independent opinions, struck four and took five minutes over it.

The girl opened her lipstick. 'By the way, darling,' she said, 'the fish will have to go.'

'The fish?' He stared. 'What, you mean my fish?'

'Yes, darling,' she said.

Teddy's eyes turned fondly to the tank of tropical fish, its water bubbling away inoffensively over his bookcase. He'd started the collection in his study at school, at the sacrifice of countless L.P. records, Coca-Colas, and haircuts. They'd been his constant companions ever since, like Bo-Peep's sheep. He found them absolutely fascinating, particularly the cunning ones you could see right the way through. He even fancied he'd managed to teach them some elementary little tricks. Odd, you may think, for anyone to get so attached to the little beasts. But with some people it's dogs. With Teddy it happened to be fish.

'Go?' he asked blankly. 'Go where?'

'The Serpentine or Mac Fisheries' slab or wherever you like, darling. But I'm not sharing a home with them and you.'

'On the contrary, Abigail.' He stiffened, hardly believing the girl was calmly making up her face and handing his friends notice to quit. 'I definitely regard those fish as part of my trousseau.'

She shut her lipstick with a snap. 'And I definitely refuse to decorate my drawing-room with fish.'

'Oh, that's all right then. I was planning to keep them in the bedroom.'

'The bedroom?'

He nodded. 'Yes, watching them flitting gently to and fro helps me to drop off. I'm sure they're ever so much better for you than sleeping pills.'

She jumped up. 'Do I understand you intend me to take my clothes off every night under the eyes of a tankful of fish?'

'That strikes me as perfectly reasonable.'

11

She raised her eyebrows as he put down his foot. 'That strikes *me* as perfectly disgusting.'

'Damn it, Abigail!' Teddy burst out. 'Don't you know it's a sign of civilization, being kind to dumb animals?'

'Oh? Indeed?' She spurned him on to greater heights. 'Then in that case you can count me among the barbarians.'

'Really! If you've developed some unhealthy persecution complex about my fish, I can only say it's high time you went along to a psychiatrist and had your sanity examined.'

'I am not referring to your fish.' She advanced on him like a well-groomed tigress with a lunch appointment. 'I am referring to you.'

'Me?'

'Yes.' She gathered her bag. 'I have been licking your boots long enough. The feet of clay are beginning to show through. As far as I am concerned you can climb in the tank with your beastly fish, and I hope everyone forgets your ants' eggs.'

'Here—' He got to his feet. 'Where are you going?'

'Home, by the next train. And if you dare to follow me, Mr. Brickwood, or even pick up a telephone to call me—in fact, if you have the temerity in future to think of me at all, I shall scream so loudly it will echo all the way from Berkeley Square to Scotland Yard. Your ring.'

She tossed it among the tea things.

12

'Abigail,' Teddy pointed out, quivering rather, 'you may regret this.'

She laughed, like a blunt circular saw striking a knot. 'If I do, I shall send round to Fortnum's for a basket of sour grapes. Good afternoon.'

She pulled on her gloves. She tipped up her nose. She swept out.

'And I haven't heard from her since,' ended Teddy, giving his father an account of the *tête-à-tête*.

Mr. Brickwood emitted a howl, upsetting the *crêpes Suzettes* again.

'You idiot!' he cried. 'You fool! Didn't you try to stop her? Didn't you run after her? What are you? A man or an emasculated mouse?'

Teddy shrugged his shoulders. 'I suppose I was too overcome for a moment to move,' he confessed.

Fact is, the poor fellow had simply stood there, feeling like Romeo if Juliet had shoved him off the balcony and then laughed like stink at his fractured leg. Wild sensations of unreality had swept over him. But there was the ring, glinting in the butter. And all that was left of Abigail was a rather expensive smell.

'You will take a taxi and go straight round to Berkeley Square and apologize,' barked Mr. Brickwood, poking a finger.

'No, Father,' returned Teddy sombrely. 'I've been thinking it over, and I feel it's all for the best. Those few moments revealed a most

13

unpleasant trait in Abigail's character, and I—'

'You will beg that woman's forgiveness on bended knee,' shouted Mr. Brickwood. 'You haven't pawned the ring yet?' he added nervously.

'It's very good of you, Father, always thinking about my future, but—'

'Damn it, you moron! It's not your blasted future I'm thinking about. It's mine.'

Teddy frowned. 'Yours? But you're not marrying Abigail?'

'You dolt! I was absolutely banking on her father putting money into my firm.'

'Money?' Teddy seemed dazed. 'But surely, Brickwood and Vole is the most old established independent London publishing house?'

'Yes, you half-wit, and like every other independent London publishing house we're broke.'

'Broke?'

'Impoverished. Insolvent. As much in the red as a wasp in raspberry jam.'

'But ... but...' He indicated the lush spectacle of people building themselves up on their expense accounts. 'All this—'

'Fringe benefits,' said his father impatiently. 'Tell her it was all a mistake. Explain you'd had a nervous breakdown. Fix the wedding. Next Thursday suits me, if it's all right.'

Teddy sat up. He felt like George Washington owning up about the cherry tree and then

14

finding his dad after him with the axe. 'I will not,' he declared quietly. 'Not after she was so beastly to me. Not to mention my fish.'

'Oh? So it doesn't matter to you if I've got one foot in the grave and the other on the Official Receiver's doormat? You're going to marry Abigail Fitzhammond.'

'I certainly am not.'

'You're nothing but a callous and ungrateful young man,' shouted Mr. Brickwood, now completely ruining the *crêpes Suzettes*.

'In that case I wouldn't make her much of a husband, would I?'

'Listen to me— Where are you going?'

'Thank you for a very nice lunch, Father.' Teddy rose with dignity. 'But now I must be off. I've got to find somewhere to kennel the fish.'

'Come back, you young hound!'

'Good day, Father.'

He strode from the restaurant. The last he heard was a roar behind him of, 'Waiter! Bring me a bottle of brandy and Whitaker's *Almanack*.

CHAPTER THREE

Personally, I shouldn't have cared much to marry Abigail Fitzhammond, even though she was a tall slim brunette with legs as trim as a pair of freshly sharpened pencils. It was the old case of one man's mate being another man's poison. But young Teddy regarded her as coming straight from heaven, with his name on the label.

'George!' he'd exclaimed, catching sight of his friend at Oxford as the Michaelmas Term started the autumn before. 'I am the happiest man in the world.'

'Oh, hello, Teddy. I'm delighted to hear it,' returned George Churchyard.

They'd met in the College gateway, which was gay with the flutter of coloured notices announcing all manner of Oxford activities from madrigals to Marxism, and littered with piles of trunks, bicycles, and rather bemused freshmen.

'I am going to be married to the most wonderful woman ever created,' Teddy explained.

He expanded this for ten minutes. You know how chaps get in the circumstances.

'And where,' George managed to get in at last, 'did you meet this exceptional creature?'

'I picked her up in Trafalgar Square.'

'Ah, tut,' said George.

He knew the Brickwood family prided itself on a broadminded tolerance towards the little failings and eccentricities of human nature which elsewhere would raise eyebrows like rocketing pheasants. But George felt this introduction, though fair enough for the start of a gay undergraduate evening, was hardly the first solemn step towards the altar.

'You just picked her up?' he added, a touch severely.

George was older than Teddy Brickwood, his father having gone out to be a professor in Australia and already getting his son processed once in the academic mill at Sydney University.

'Yes, one Sunday afternoon.'

'H'm.'

'It all happened last July. I was getting frightfully bored sitting alone in the old man's flat in Eton Square,' Teddy recounted, as they strolled across the quadrangle while a small bell somewhere raised its voice for evening Chapel. 'You know what London's like on Sunday? About as lively as a wet night at Stonehenge. I thought I'd take a stroll in the sunshine, and I wandered past the Palace and down the Mall thinking of nothing in particular, when I suddenly found a beautiful girl lying on the pavement at my feet. Naturally, I thought she'd been run over by a taxi or something, and helped her up. She went limp in my arms. You

17

can't imagine what a thrilling experience it was.'

'You mean it was vertigo?'

'No, it was one of those Ban the Bomb rallies. When she discovered I wasn't a policeman I had to put her down again of course. But there was a chap playing the guitar next to her who very decently offered me a seat. Right from the start Abigail and I got on splendidly,' Teddy recalled warmly, as they reached his staircase. 'The upshot was that while everyone else was being carted off to Bow Street I carted her off for a cup of tea in Lyons' Corner House, and a fortnight later we decided to get married.'

George naturally uncorked the congratulations.

'There is at the moment,' Teddy added sombrely, 'only one obstacle in the way of our future happiness.'

'She's doing time in Holloway?'

'No. Money.'

'Oh, come,' George protested. 'You may think you're pretty stony up here at Oxford. But the scholarly life is never compatible with ritzing it up. Your old man must be pretty well breeched, surely? Just look at the booze the authors got through at his last literary party.'

'Not my money. Hers. She's Abigail Fitzhammond.'

'What, the daughter of the great shipping chap who keeps taking over things?'

Teddy nodded.

George gave a low whistle. He couldn't see how that was any objection unless the girl looked like the back of a bus, and then a pretty battered old bus it would have to be.

'I was at school with her brother Fabian,' George remembered. 'Tell me, is it true the old boy reads balance sheets in bed?'

'I refuse to have my way oiled by the Fitzhammond millions,' Teddy continued, throwing out his chest so hard he pretty near cracked his costal cartilages. 'As for Abigail, she says one should never lose touch with The People. She absolutely despises money,' he ended. 'She's an extraordinary girl.'

'Extraordinary,' George agreed with him whole-heartedly.

Though it's not all that unusual for a tycoon's daughter, who usually looked as if she'd just come from Hardy Amies via Cartier's, to be found sitting in Trafalgar Square. I mean, you've only got to look at the Bow Street charge sheet over the past few years. I suppose it's the only way left for the posher daughters to get their photos in the papers, now that they've stopped having debutantes.

But the path of true love turned into a cul-de-sac, and there was Teddy stalking out of the restaurant, leaving his father eyeing the vacant chair like a patch of grass recently vacated by its snake.

It was a wonderful afternoon outside—one of

19

those glorious May days when England stirs in the first coy glances of the sun like a matronly Sleeping Beauty, as motor-mowers chatter happily to each other once again across back fences, the bird sings blithely on the telly aerial, and the very gnomes on front lawns seem to be exchanging winks. Out in the country the bees and the blossom were doing their stuff and the early bluebells appeared in the cyclists' saddle-bags, down by the sea the landladies were turning their mattresses, and even the grey streets of London where Teddy now stalked were cheered with signs of the awakening year, as the busmen went on strike against their summer schedules and Abigail's chums started marching down Whitehall prophesying nuclear doom all round tomorrow.

Teddy strode down Piccadilly, blind to the lunchtime crowds all looking as gay as something out of Walt Disney. He pulled up on spotting a placard announcing FAMOUS TV PERSONALITY DIES, and hastily bought a paper wondering if Nemesis had done an efficient job on Professor Needler. But he found only a paragraph among the jolly police court jokes recounting the demise of some unfortunate chap who'd once made a thing of it playing *The Last Chord* on a saw, and throwing the paper away wandered aimlessly until he discovered himself in St. James's Park. He spotted an empty bench and sat down. He tried to look for the silver lining, and found it as thin as the chrome on a modern production car.

A few days before he had been in possession of a promising career, a beautiful fiancée, and a fond and prosperous parent. Now all three seemed to have disappeared like icebergs in the Gulf Stream. Life seemed to him as confusing and mysterious as *Waiting for Godot*. For you must remember that Teddy, though as an ambassador could probably have sold Metternich the three-card trick, was still a young sprig who didn't entirely *savoir* how to *faire*.

His eyes strayed to the Foreign Office, just past the pelicans, its doors forever barred to him. He didn't feel particularly sorry. And I can't say I blame him, because I once knew a chap in the Diplomatic Service, and though it must be no end of fun lashing up some foreign War Minister's mistress with champagne while she extracts the plans of the latest ballistic missile from the top of her stocking, that comes only after years and years of sweating it out in Whitehall wearing a stiff collar and writing everything in triplicate.

Teddy's tender mind, reared on purest academic milk, searched among the harsh possibilities of alternative employment. He secretly felt he'd written some pretty killing stuff for *The Abattoir*, not to mention that splitting account in the mag, of someone breaking a leg in the Fathers' Match which got him beaten at school. He'd also finished a jolly biting play about the follies of the elderly people of this world, over the age of forty. But he was a level-headed young man who realized that before he was taken for the author of *Gulliver's Travels* there was a good deal of leeway to be made up. Though the fact is, the chap was no more satirical at heart than Enid Blyton. He was just a healthy young man who liked to say ya-boo at the beaks, and he fitted into the modern trend as snugly as into his jeans.

Teddy sat pondering for some time, exchanging glances with a rather inquisitive pigeon. He felt that at least Professor Needler had cleared the decks of life a bit. Leaving Oxford in George Churchyard's MG that morning, they'd weighed the chances of Mr. Brickwood's putting up capital for a new satirical nightclub. Now, of course, there was as much possibility of Mr Brickwood's putting up capital for oil prospecting on Clapham Common. One job on the vacancy list struck him as saving the family fortunes, by picking Brickwood and Vole from the gutter and dusting them down. He could dedicate himself to this task, he decided firmly, particularly now he was freed from a highly unwise female entanglement.

He suddenly felt chilly, and glancing at his watch was surprised to find it already six o'clock. He stood up. A more immediate problem in life was finding somewhere to spend the night. It seemed best to avoid Eaton Square, and his father coming home in the mood of Herod the Great with the effects of a bottle of brandy wearing off.

CHAPTER FOUR

'Father,' announced Teddy, 'I'm sorry.'

'Oh, hello, my boy.' Mr. Brickwood looked up from the evening paper in his penthouse flat in Eaton Square, the sort of place they kept photographing for magazines to instruct suburban readers how to go about gracious living. It's always been a mystery to me how so many people in London manage to go broke in luxury.

'Of course, it's no concern of mine,' his father went on, 'but where have you been spending the past few nights? Somewhere quite comfortable, I hope?'

'I found a little hotel place round the back of the British Museum. Rum coves appeared at breakfast, but it was all right.'

'I looked for you outside that restaurant,' Mr. Brickwood told him amiably. 'It occurred to me you might be about to throw yourself into the Thames or the arms of undesirable women.

23

Strange in London, isn't it? The people you want to see disappear faster than taxis in a shower, while the ones you definitely don't are lurking round every corner. If you want a shakedown here, there's plenty of room,' he added. 'You'll join me for dinner, at any rate?'

'I thought it about time I returned to the family bosom,' said Teddy awkwardly. He was a dutiful and considerate lad at heart, and besides there was only thirty bob left in the rather nice crocodile wallet Abigail had given him for Christmas. 'I'm afraid I haven't behaved towards you exactly the way a son should,' he confessed, settling on the edge of a mustard-yellow leather armchair.

'On the contrary, Teddy,' Mr. Brickwood turned a page. 'You behaved exactly as I should have expected any clean-minded, red-blooded young man to react in the circumstances. To put sordid commercial considerations before my son's happiness was totally inexcusable. I was behaving like Mr. Barrett of Wimpole Street's little brother. Pray let us not discuss this distressing but nevertheless quite trivial matter any further.'

He went back to his paper.

'I'm sorry the family finances have collapsed like an underdone soufflé,' Teddy went on rather more briskly. 'But I think I definitely ought to join the firm. I've already developed a simply terrific idea. Before we call in the

Salvation Army with the coal and hot soup, perhaps Uncle Horatio could be touched for a sub?'

Mr. Brickwood made a noise behind his paper like a major fault occurring in some piece of heavy machinery.

'I mean, he may have struck it frightfully rich out East,' Teddy suggested warmly.

'Why? He never struck it anything but disastrously while he was still out West.'

'But don't you remember that peculiar sailor chap who rang up last summer? With the message that Uncle Horatio was up to the armpits in Hong Kong dollars and wanted to leave his bones within his native shores? Just like *Treasure Island.*'

'Without the treasure,' snorted his father. 'Anyway, his bones are in perfectly good order. He only likes to give the impression of enormous age when its suits him. Teddy, I have been, I think, an indulgent parent. The only rules I ever set were always to clean your teeth after breakfast and never to mention the name of your uncle. Will you kindly see that they are still observed?'

'Yes, Father,' agreed Teddy meekly.

'A pity about the firm, of course,' reflected Mr. Brickwood. 'After all, we did publish Dickens. Or would have done, if the idiotic office boy hadn't left his manuscript in a hansom cab. I suppose I shall have to get myself taken over by the Americans, like everyone else. In fact, I'm already booked with B.O.A.C. for a couple of days' time, and I'm expecting hourly confirmation of my suite at the Waldorf.'

A silence fell between them. Mr. Brickwood seemed to be finding a good deal of absorbing news in his paper. Teddy took a typewritten bundle from a foot-high pile of manuscripts beside his chair, and starting browsing through a five-hundred-page American novel about the sex life of the inhabitants of some exclusive New York suburb. He was becoming interested in the executive's wife who had, poor dear, both a mother- and a father-fixation and was getting a bit larky with the bloke delivering the ice, when Mr. Brickwood observed casually from the press, 'Nice girl, Abigail.'

'Abigail? Oh, very,' Teddy concurred.

'A good-looker.'

'Yes, indeed.'

'Charming and intelligent conversationalist.'

'Certainly.'

'A young lady, I would say, of many accomplishments.'

Teddy nodded. She could get a hundred and twenty out of her Austin Healey and play the trombone at parties.

'Still, that's all over and done with,' ended Mr. Brickwood.

'I rang up the Aquarium but they didn't seem very keen,' Teddy burst out suddenly. 'About taking my fish, I mean. At the moment they're still in Oxford, with my scout sort of *in loco parentis*.'

Mr. Brickwood glanced quickly over the gold rims.

'No doubt there exists somewhere the piscine equivalent of the Battersea Dogs' Home,' he suggested helpfully. 'I recall in the days of my youth gentlemen roamed the streets of London with a horse and cart, offering children fish in jam-jars in exchange for superfluous household hardware. Possibly one may still be found, who would provide yours with a good home.'

'I can't understand why on earth we had that stupid row.' Teddy tossed the manuscript aside and started to pace about with his hands in his pockets. 'Abigail was being so terribly sensible about everything else we discussed that afternoon—the atomic age, under-privileged countries, and so on. Perhaps . . . perhaps,' he faltered, 'I made a remark about fish in the bedroom which might offend a girl's natural feelings of midesty?'

The trouble with poor old Teddy, of course, was that he didn't offend a girl's natural feelings of modesty half enough. When a young woman comes all the way to Oxford in the springtime, she doesn't much care to be fobbed off with the atomic age and the under-privileged countries.

'I've been a fool,' he announced, sitting down again.

27

Remorse was eating into his soul like a starving rat in a cheesemonger's. It's all very well for a man to shrug his shoulders as his fiancée disappears over the horizon, and wait at the stop for the next one along. After a while he begins to remember what a nice laugh she had, and what jolly times they enjoyed together, not to mention the little soft hairs at the back of her neck. And there's nothing like a few days' residence in a small hotel behind the British Museum for inducing a mood of melancholy introspection. Between touring the theatrical agencies with George Churchyard, Teddy had spent most of his time sitting on park benches gazing darkly across the sea of troubles which had so recently swamped his life. But whichever way he looked, those thundering breakers shrank to ripples against the vision of Abigail's ring in the butter. He started to develop a nasty attack of the pines.

'A fool,' he emphasized his point.

Mr. Brickwood, clued up with the day's events at last, threw his paper aside and regarded his offspring keenly.

'As I said, a father's duty is always to back up his son. It distresses me deeply to see you reduced to such a pitiful state. I will therefore give you some advice, my boy. Go round to Berkeley Square with a bunch of flowers and an offer to kiss and make up immediately.'

'No, I won't,' announced Teddy, jumping up

28

and starting all that pacing again. 'I utterly refuse to go along and grovel.'

'Dammit, man!' exclaimed his father impatiently. 'What do you expect me to do? Hire a public relations man to go and do your grovelling for you?'

'I am perfectly prepared to swallow a portion of humble pie,' declared Teddy stoutly. 'But I definitely won't risk a slice of cold shoulder on the side.'

'Really, Teddy! The way you're carrying on anyone would think you and Abigail were married already.'

'But I have a plan,' Teddy announced.

'A plan?'

'George Churchyard,' Teddy explained, 'who, lucky blighter, has landed himself a terrific job in cabaret, was at school with Abigail's brother Fabian. And he got pretty pally with both of them when they came up to Oxford now and then to see *The Abattoir*. I shall simply get George to nip down to Fabian's office in the City and find how the land lies. If Abigail has put up the emotional shutters, well, that's the end of that. But if possibly she'd like to see me just once again . . .'

'My dear Teddy, you really are a loss to the Diplomatic Service,' agreed Mr. Brickwood. 'Long before you got into Oxford I knew I was blessed with a son of remarkable perception and intelligence. Believe me, I only want to see the pair of you happy again. Send me a cable at the Waldorf once you're reunited in bliss.'

'I'll go and see George at his cabaret tonight,' Teddy decided. 'Meanwhile, I'd rather like you to fit me somehow on the pay-roll. As you know, I definitely intend to keep Abigail in the way to which she is not accustomed.'

'You can start by reading a few manuscripts for me.' The publisher indicated the foot-high pile. 'It will make an excellent introduction to the contemporary literary scene, and allow my own mind to range over the wider issues in New York. No anniversaries, I suppose?' he added, his eyes straying hopefully towards the silver calendar on the mantelpiece.

Teddy shrugged his shoulders.

'By jove, Teddy my boy! Fetch out the whisky. I've just remembered, this was the day years and years ago we finally shot off your Uncle Horatio to Hong Kong.'

CHAPTER FIVE

Teddy Brickwood let himself into the hall of the penthouse after seeing his father off at London Airport a couple of days later and stopped dead. He sniffed. The smell of cigars hung in the air. He wondered quickly if his parent had been puffing one before leaving, but it was only eleven in the morning and Mr. Brickwood maintained all his life that no gentleman smoked a cigar before lunch. It couldn't be anyone calling on his stepmother—Mr. Brickwood's wives had run to several editions—because she was still in Cannes. Possibly the char, he speculated, indulging in a *Romeo y Julieta* as she scrubbed the kitchen floor? Or perhaps the better sort of burglar, as you'd expect in Eaton Square? He pushed open the drawing-room door.

'Oh, I'm frightfully sorry,' Teddy exclaimed.

He had clearly stumbled into the wrong flat. Sitting in an armchair with an open box of cigars and a decanter of whisky at his elbow was a grey-haired, well-dressed, plumpish, monocled gentleman with the air of jovial prosperity of the Man Who Broke the Bank at Monte Carlo.

'Great heavens!' exclaimed the gentleman. 'It is.'

'I must have got the wrong floor,' mumbled Teddy, backing towards the hall.

'Of course it is! It couldn't be anyone else.' The visitor advanced on him. 'Surely it must be? Isn't it?'

'Very confusing, these flats—'

'It's dear little Teddy.'

'I beg your pardon?'

'Come now! Come and kiss your Nunky.'

'Good lord—you—you're—?'

'Yes, perhaps you're a bit old for that,'

31

conceded Lord Brickwood. 'Have a cigar instead.'

Teddy stared at him. Uncle Horatio's photograph had for reasons never fully explained been pretty heavily censored from the family archives, but he seemed to remember somewhere the picture of a slim young chap on a horse. It struck him wildly this fellow might be some impostor, but he'd gathered that if people wanted to go about pretending to be members of the family Lord Brickwood would come pretty low on the list of impersonations.

'How did you get in?' was all he could think of saying.

'That porter fellow. Susceptible to bribes. I should have him sacked. My dear Teddy,' went on Lord Brickwood, grasping his hand. 'My most heartfelt congratulations.'

'Congratulations?' He looked blank. 'On what?'

'Your impending marriage, of course. Such a delightful and sensible choice you have made. I learned the joyous news by mere chance just three days ago. Dropping into Maxim's Bar in Hong Kong for my morning nourishment, I happened to spot your charming fiancée's photograph in a back number of the *Tatler*. Naturally, I hopped on a plane and came home at once. The wedding is pretty soon, I gather?'

'Oh, yes, soon,' Teddy mumbled. 'Quite soon.'

For all the news he'd had from George Churchyard since sending him on his delicate mission, the chap might have been fired into outer space. Teddy quickly decided to say nothing. When an uncle comes half-way round the earth for the purpose of downing iced cake and champers at your wedding and then finds the event has been cancelled through lack of support, he may feel justifiably narked.

'And now,' added Lord Brickwood, stylishly flicking his cigar over an ashtray, 'where is my dear, dear brother?'

'Good heavens!' Teddy jumped. 'But I've just seen Father off to New York from London Airport.'

'Really?' remarked Lord Brickwood, not seeming particularly disappointed. 'He must have been channelled in one direction while I was being channelled in the other. My own fault, of course. I was always a wretched correspondent. But the sight of a blank sheet of writing paper always has a paralysing effect on logical thought. It was anyway well worth the journey to set eyes on you again, young man,' he continued fondly. 'It seems but a moment since you were mewling and puking all over the shop. I left you my sweet coupons, by the way.'

'Thank you, Uncle,' murmured Teddy politely, wondering what on earth to do next.

'A pleasant room,' went on Uncle Horatio, looking round smilingly. 'What's through

33

there?'

'That door? It leads to the dining-room and a largish kitchen,' Teddy informed him. 'Through the dining-room is a corridor giving off four beds and baths, and so on.'

'A charming little *pied-à-terre*,' Lord Brickwood dismissed the family home. 'How delightful London becomes when the hounds of spring are sniffing round winter's lamp posts,' he reflected, gazing through the window at Eaton Square and the trees bursting impatiently into their fresh green summer dresses. 'Though I fear I shall hardly recognize the West End any longer. Not now they've turned up all the lights and turned out all the girls. But come, my boy! After twenty years stewing in the tropics I refuse to waste another second of this charming day. Let us take luncheon at my club. I hope you've no other engagement?'

Teddy assured him he was free from any commitments whatever.

'Excellent!' Lord Brickwood took up grey homburg, yellow gloves, and silver-headed cane. 'I only hope the place is still there. Max Beerbohm once wrote a heart-rending story about a fellow who survived exile only by contemplating his first whisky and soda on returning to his London club—but alas, they were just knocking down the last chimney stack. And we can easily get a cab,' he added, descending in the lift. 'You can't imagine how complicated life was, Teddy, before I left the Army and started afresh in the wider horizons out East. You couldn't find a decent bottle of champagne and the Americans had commandeered all the taxis.'

'But I thought they were on our side?' asked Teddy, confused.

'Yes, I suppose they were, really,' murmured Lord Brickwood, making for the front door and waving his silver-topped cane. 'Pall Mall,' he commanded the driver.

Lord Brickwood spent the journey remarking on all the new buildings which are shooting up in London like asparagus. Teddy sat silently in the corner of the cab, feeling as if some fabulous beast had appeared in Eaton Square and started nuzzling him. He had heard little about his uncle over the years, Lord Brickwood's name automatically stopping the conversation whenever it was mentioned. But he gathered the chap was some kind of financial wizard, and Teddy had to admit he seemed as much the embodiment of prosperity as the capitalists with top hats in the cartoons, leaning back fingering his old school tie, glancing at his slim gold pocket-watch, and giving a sniff to the carnation in his buttonhole.

'We have ample time for a leisurely luncheon,' Lord Brickwood observed with satisfaction. 'I believe one can define a gentleman as someone who is never in a hurry, don't you? Afterwards,' he added, 'perhaps you will introduce me to this beautiful fiancée of yours?'

'She's—she's away at the moment,' countered Teddy quickly. 'Just for a few days.'

He wondered nervously what on earth George Churchyard was up to. Apart from the reunion in bliss angle, he now had to produce a living and breathing fiancée for his uncle, and look pretty damn smart about it, too.

'Oh? How unfortunate. But I should have guessed. You seem a shade morose for a young man shortly to be married. You can rely on me, my boy, to keep your mind occupied and cheerful until she comes back.' Uncle Horatio slapped his nephew on the knee. 'But aren't you up at Oxford, or something? That must be utterly delightful. Glorious weeks of drifting down the Isis in punts, with girls who seem created only for a summer afternoon's love-making, like the mayfly,' he expanded. 'Though as I recall, some of them turned out rather more like gnats.'

'I decided I was wasting my time up there,' Teddy explained briefly. 'They make you work pretty grimly these days, you know.'

'In that case I don't blame you for getting out. Frightful intellectual closed shops, these universities. Life is the best teacher of them all, take it from me. Though the fees on occasion come somewhat expensive.' He rapped on the

36

glass partition with his cane. 'Here will do, driver. Dear old Pall Mall,' Lord Brickwood exclaimed, paying the cab off. 'It looks exactly the same. You can't imagine how one dreams of this wonderful London soot. You know, I feel just like Rip van Winkle trying to make his number again with the neighbours.' He gave a chuckle like port gurgling into a decanter. 'It's so long since I left I must confess I have no idea exactly which my club is.' His eyes travelled along the line of anonymous buildings, each apparently built to last as long as the Pyramids. 'This one, I fancy,' he added, indicating with his stick the massive door opposite. 'I expect you are not unaware of its name?'

'Yes, the Trafalgar,' Teddy nodded, pleased to give a flash of worldliness.

'That's exactly right,' agreed Lord Brickwood, bounding up the front steps. 'Good morning, porter,' he greeted the man in the little glass cubicle. 'A good many years since I set foot in the place. I'll wager you don't even recognize me any longer.'

'Of course I recognize you, sir,' replied the porter quickly. 'I always recgonize all the members, sir.'

'Twenty years, George—it is George, isn't it?'

'Charles, sir. George retired some time back.'

'Charles, of course. I was always muddling you up. You're much younger than George, of course.'

'Can give him a few summers, sir,' smiled the porter.

'Duke of Essex been in much recently?'

'His Grace passed on a good time ago now, sir.'

'What, dear old Rudolph?' Teddy's uncle was aghast. 'Dear me! How one misses these items out East. We were so very close at one time.' He blew his nose on a yellow silk handkerchief. 'But it must come to all of us, I suppose. Where do I put my hat?'

'Just on the right, sir.'

'Thank you, Charles.'

'By the way, sir—the name is of course . . .'

'Lord Brickwood.'

'Sorry, my Lord. It just slipped my memory for the second.'

'No trouble at all, Charles.'

'I always pride myself, my Lord, I can place every single member.'

'Of course, Charles. That's what a club porter is for. Don't give it another thought. The smoking-room, if I recall, is straight ahead? Come, Teddy. It is a proud moment, I assure you, for me to entertain you, as a grown man, for the very first time as a guest in my club.'

They went inside.

CHAPTER SIX

The Trafalgar Club was raised on foundations of Victorian confidence in the British Empire, and had lasted a good deal better. It had hundreds of members and an air of solid spacious dinginess, like King's Cross Station. The décor ran a good deal to huge tawny oil-paintings and marble statues of upstage goddesses clutching draperies round them in alcoves, as though hearing the telephone in the shower. Possibly some of those Dickensian fogs had once seeped in and never got out again, because however hard the sun shone in Pall Mall outside the Trafalgar Club always enjoyed an atmosphere of underwater gloom, laced with the smells of old, dead dinners long ago.

Lord Brickwood paused in the main hall, from which you'd gather membership was confined to rather sportive giants, the place being large enough to house three or four families pretty comfortably in prefabs, and lined with pillars that would have made old Samson sweat a bit.

'As I thought.' Lord Brickwood turned to the tape machine which was chattering away to itself behind the brass and mahogany hat racks. 'Associated Carborundums are up a couple of points. They'll split, mark my words. I'd pick up a few if I were you, Teddy, before it's too late.'

Teddy thanked him.

'Ah, the smoking-room,' Uncle Horatio announced, entering an apartment which struck Teddy as being the size of the Albert Hall. 'Nothing has changed,' he went on admiringly, running his monocle round the portraits of old gentlemen with shocking blood pressures decorating the walls. 'Even the gout stools are poised ready for action, I note. Here should do nicely.'

They took a couple of armchairs designed for weary elephants. An arthritic waiter materialized himself, and Uncle Horatio ordered champagne in specially iced tankards.

'Tell me all about the charming Miss Fitzhammond,' Lord Brickwood went on, as Teddy sipped his champagne wondering if all those rumours about his uncle were just the little bits of gossip you get in any family. 'I'm absolutely dying to meet her. And her family, of course. Her father, now—he resides permanently in London, I take it?'

Teddy replied, rather cunningly he thought, 'But Uncle, I wish you'd tell me some of you own adventures out East. Have you been all this time in Hong Kong?'

'Macao mostly.' Lord Brickwood made a vague gesture of his tankard. 'The Portuguese colony, you know. So much more restful than

Hong Kong. Nothing but bustle and cocktail parties there from morning to night—'

He broke off. Something stirred in the armchair opposite. A thin, white-haired member had been woken by their conversation from the trance in which I suppose he had suspended himself since breakfast.

'Great heavens above,' exclaimed Lord Brickwood, as the figure became distinguishable through the gloom. 'Surely it can't be old—'

He rose, and grasped the man's hand.

'You haven't changed a bit,' Lord Brickwood declared warmly.

'Wassat?' asked the fellow member, cupping an ear.

'I said you hadn't changed a scrap,' Lord Brickwood shouted.

'Someone will come if you ring the bell.'

'Surely you remember me? Horatio Brickwood.'

The white-haired old boy shook his head. 'Sorry. Wrong chap. I'm General Gowing.'

'No, no, *I* am Horatio Brickwood, General. Haven't been in the Club for years. How's the old complaint?' he added more loudly.

A light came into the General's eye, as though contemplating battles long ago.

'Not so good.'

'I'm sorry to hear it,' roared Lord Brickwood.

'It's the back,' the General informed him.

'Yes, it always was, wasn't it?'

41

'Right at the base of the neck.'

'Hasn't moved an inch, eh?'

'Doctor feller can't do anything.'

'Rotten luck.'

'Tried every one in Harley Street.'

'Don't trust 'em myself.'

The General was about to launch into the strategy and tactics of his campaign against the back, when another figure swam into view through the murk.

'Sir George Peach,' the old boy introduced politely, though sounding pretty disappointed. After all, everyone else in the club had been hearing for years about his ruddy back.

'I don't think I quite caught your—'

'Lord Brickwood,' said Lord Brickwood.

'I think we lunched here together the other day,' murmured Sir George politely.

'Alas! That shows how time flies. I have been abroad for some years. Business, you know. But I hope we can take luncheon together very shortly. It would so help me to pick up the threads. Or perhaps a game of cards one evening . . .?'

'You'll find me ready for a rubber any time except before breakfast,' smiled Sir George.

'Indeed?' Lord Brickwood's eye lit up at discovering a playmate. 'I am quite devoted to the card table. Perhaps you'd care to drop round to my place one evening with a few friends? The stakes allowed in these clubs are so derisory.

Now I must leave you for an early lunch. My young nephew here'—he indicated Teddy, who had been sitting pretty overwhelmed by all this—'has a busy afternoon planned for me in London, I'm sure. Delighted to meet you again, Peach. How's the old complaint?'

'Always comes on a bit at this time of the year,' returned Sir George, rubbing his shoulder.

'Yes, it does, doesn't it? I'm sure it will soon be greatly improved. Come, Teddy. The dining-room is upstairs, of course?'

The food at the Trafalgar Club was like the architecture, designed for durability rather than attractiveness. Teddy munched his way through steak and kidney pie, listening eagerly to his uncle's anecdotes about wartime London life, most of which seemed to concern Poles.

'I hope you can accompany me on some errands?' asked Lord Brickwood, as he paid the bill and they descended the marble staircase. 'I mean, you haven't got some beastly office to attend, or anything?'

'No, I'm pretty free,' admitted Teddy. 'Father's left me a few manuscripts to criticize, that's all.'

'I'm so glad. Nothing is more harmful to a spirited young man than regular work. It shrivels the soul like lemon on an oyster. I always believe—'

'Lord Brickwood.' The porter stuck his head

43

from the glass box as Uncle Horatio reached for his hat.

'Yes, Charles?'

'Sorry to disturb you, my Lord, but it seems there's been a bit of a mistake. Your name's been left out from the list of members.'

'Has it, by jove!' Lord Brickwood's eyebrows shot up. 'I shall certainly have a word with the Secretary about this.'

'I'm very sorry, my Lord.'

'I suppose it is understandable,' admitted Uncle Horatio loftily. 'I arranged with my bankers to pay some sort of lump subscription before the war.'

'All the Club records were bombed, my Lord.'

'Ah! That certainly explains it.' Lord Brickwood rubbed his hands. 'I won't bother the Secretary after all. See I'm included in next year's list.'

'Very good, my Lord.'

'Thank you, Charles. And Charles—'

'Yes, my Lord?'

'How's the old complaint?' asked Lord Brickwood.

CHAPTER SEVEN

While Teddy Brickwood was being solidly lunched at the Trafalgar Club, George Churchyard was dutifully bringing himself to call at Fabian Fitzhammond's office to fly his courting kite for him. George hadn't taken much to the idea.

'You were jolly lucky to land a job in this cabaret, I must say,' Teddy had begun when they'd met, a couple of evenings before, backstage at the Harem Club.

'Yes, the fellow who usually tells the gags has just got run in for being rude in Leicester Square,' George explained. 'Though I feel I've rather dropped my *avant-garde*,' he confessed.

'Do you give them the one about the Red Indian Chief?'

George nodded. 'Not that it goes over like at Oxford. In fact, it's a pretty discouraging show altogether. As soon as I appear between the strippers, all those bald heads facing you like a case of packing-station eggs rise as a man and make for the bar.'

The Harem Club wasn't one of those flashy joints, all plush hangings, liveried waiters, and overpriced champagne. It was a simple little place you'd hardly notice in an alley off Greek Street, between a rather olfactory Italian grocer's and one of those bookshops which would make a field day for the Institute of Psychiatrists. The front door was just past the dustbins of a Chinese restaurant, a bit tricky to get at with all those beansprouts and bamboo-shoots underfoot, and decorated with a couple of photographs of girls striking you as pretty chilly in the London climate. Inside it was equally modest, with parish hall chairs and canteen tables, and a good many notices setting the tone by forbidding gambling, drinking out of bottles, chucking lighted cigarettes at the performers, and gentlemen dancing together.

George Churchyard, like young Lupin Pooter, always had secret ambitions to go on the stage, a career appealing to a good many young men through offering advantages such as having all day off and making love to beautiful actresses in the line of duty. He'd been hoping to start with something more in the satirical way, but touring the theatrical agencies in Shaftesbury Avenue he'd discovered that London was crawling with bright young men who could imitate Prime Ministers. The few rapier-like wits who first cut into the conventions of the day seemed to have turned into a charge of fixed bayonets. Admittedly, he told himself, he'd done better than Teddy, but he felt his soul had been sponged with the vinegar of disillusionment.

'This is Doris.' George introduced Teddy to a

shimmering blonde in an old pink dressing-gown, sitting on an orange box with a cup of Ovaltine. 'How's the chest tonight, dear?'

'Real shocking,' Doris answered thickly. 'Stay out of draughts and keep yourself well wrapped up, the doctor says. I ask you!'

'Perhaps they might let you keep your vest on, or something,' he added helpfully. 'After all, the lighting's so terrible no one would notice.'

'That lot out there want their money's worth,' grumbled Doris, putting down her cup. 'You ought to have heard the row the night my zipper jammed. Like the electric hare getting stuck at the dogs, it was. Who's your nice friend?'

'We were at Oxford together,' Teddy explained.

'Coo, I say,' replied Doris, fluttering her two-inch eyelashes like a couple of startled starlings.

'One moment,' interrupted George.

He went on stage to announce Doris as Seductive Sonia from Snowy Sweden, the Icicle with the Core of Fire, while the men on the piano and drums woke from their trance to strike up Grieg's Piano Concerto.

'Just time for a quick chat,' George nodded, returning. 'Doris takes eight minutes dead to get down to bed-rock. That's Bewitching Carlotta from Glamorous Chile,' he indicated, as a snub-nosed brunette in another old dressing-gown brushed past. 'Actually, she hails from

Penge and thinks Chile's in Siberia anyway.'

As Sonia stripped, Teddy unfolded his plan for the reunion in bliss. George listened pretty cagily. Personally, he felt he'd rather wade into a scrap between a couple of hydrophobic dogs any day than meddle with somebody's love affairs. But nothing cements a friendship like mutual misfortune, and in memory of Professor Needler he'd finally agreed.

'All right, I'll give Fabian a ring at his money-making factory and make a date,' he promised, as the piano and drums finished with Grieg. 'Want to stay for the next act?' he invited. 'Fascinating Fatima from Mysterious Siam. Actually, she turned yellow working in some sort of gunpowder factory.'

Arriving for his appointment at Fitzhammond Enterprises Ltd, George was taken up in the executives' lift up to his old classmate's airy office on the top floor. Perched on the desk was a girl with a figure like the models in slimming-food advertisements, with long blond hair, knee-length green boots and jerkin to match, and dangling a string of beads resembling monkeys' heads.

'Meet Morag Aspinall,' introduced Fabian Fitzhammond, who himself ran a good deal to double-breasted waistcoats and sidewhiskers.

'Hello, darling,' said the slimming ad. girl huskily. She turned on George a pair of eyes so lavished with make-up he wondered for a

moment if she were a recent victim of assault
and battery.

'I've just given Morag a job in one of our
cruise ships,' the young tycoon went on
brightly, swivelling in his chair and putting up
his feet by his telephones. 'As hostess,' he
explained. 'I'm trying to infuse a few new ideas
into the business, now the old man's put me in
charge of the social side of our ships and hotels.
He seems to think I've got talents in that
direction.'

'Don't we all, darling,' murmured Morag.

'Morag's an interior decorator, actually,'
Fabian added, 'but her parties are out of this
world.'

'The last one was utterly cosmic,' agreed
Morag throatily.

'George Churchyard and I were lads
together,' grinned Fabian at his new employee.
'Many's a tin of sardines and bottle of fizzy cider
we've shared in the still watches. Don't you ever
go to the old school reunions, George?'

'A tribal ritual best avoided, I feel.'

'How I agree with you. Sitting digesting that
ghastly plastic chicken, while the Head Beak
enlivens the proceedings by reading out those
called to the Higher Life in the twelve months.
Then the dear old school songs and the Bishop
blubbing into his port. Ugh! Not for
Fitzhammond, I'm afraid. But I say, aren't you
up at Oxford?' He offered a gold cigarette box,

49

with a sigh. 'I do so wish I'd had the intelligence to get into a university.'

'I left Oxford,' explained George warily. 'I had a chance to go on the stage.'

'Thrilling,' purred Morag, crossing her green boots.

'Yes, I remember now,' Fabian nodded. 'After your Oedipus the school mag. said Sir Laurence had better start looking to his laurels. And you absolutely slayed me as Charley's Aunt.' He gave a slight frown. 'But I don't seem to have noticed anything in the papers?'

'I've gone in for cabaret,' George told him quickly, a bit distracted by those green boots. 'More intimate, you know.'

'Oh, really? Which night-club? I'm a member of most in Town.'

'I don't expect you'd know it. It really is very intimate indeed.'

'But Fabian, darling!' Morag swung her monkeys' heads. 'Hasn't he just dropped from heaven?'

Fabian looked puzzled.

'The entertainer, darling. He looks *terribly* entertaining to me.' Morag gave George a bit of a glance and did the boot trick again.

'By jove, yes!' The young executive snapped his fingers. 'You couldn't tear yourself away for a couple of weeks, I suppose, George? We're short of a First Class entertainer on board the *Snowdonia* for her spring cruise. All we can get from the agencies seem to be conjurers and acrobats.'

'Naturally, I'm very booked up—'

'It would be a terrific fortnight's holiday, with pay. Though you'll have to leave tomorrow, I'm afraid.'

'Perhaps I could manage for you, Fabian,' hazarded George, having of course already signed mentally on the dotted line. Apart from anything else, Doris was starting to get fond.

'That's splendid! There'll be a few tedious forms to fill up in the Marine Superintendent's office downstairs, but Janet here will show you the way,' he added as another girl with a slimming-food figure appeared with a notebook.

'Captain Kettlehorn has been waiting half an hour already in the Passenger Manager's room, Mr. Fabian,' Janet announced.

Fabian groaned. 'What sort of state is he in?'

'Well he *is* going rather pink, Mr. Fabian. And his eyebrows *are* rather bristling like barbed-wire entanglements.'

'What a life! Sorry to shoo you out,' Fabian apologized wearily to the others, giving Morag's hand a quick squeeze. 'But business, you know...' he sighed again. 'Never a moment for anything else. So glad you looked in, George. Got a car? Good. You can dump it in our garage at Southampton and give Morag a lift. Take care of her, won't you? She's terribly delicate.'

'Utter Dresden,' cooed Morag.

It was only at the door George remembered. 'Here, I say! About your sister Abigail—'

'Abigail?' Fabian looked up from signing cheques. 'She's had the most frightful fit of the sulks since your pal Teddy jilted her.'

'Well, he's now sprouting at the ears with olive-branches.'

'Thank heavens for that. You can't imagine how she's getting the family down, going about looking like an obituary column. 'Bye, Morag,' he added, as she fluttered her three-inch purple nails in his direction. 'Send me a postcard from Gibraltar.'

'Thanks for the job,' added George.

He felt he had perhaps not pressed Teddy's suit as strongly as he might. But it was jolly difficult launching out about tortured souls and so on to a young executive executing in all directions as busily as Fabian Fitzhammond. And that wasn't to mention those green boots.

'Show Captain Kettlehorn straight up, will you Janet?' Fabian ended briskly.

'Yes, Mr. Fabian.'

'Oh, and Janet—'

'Yes, Mr. Fabian?'

'Stand by for rescue operations if it sounds I'm being shipwrecked.'

CHAPTER EIGHT

Dear Father, wrote Teddy Brickwood in capitals. He paused. At half-a-crown a word or whatever 'Dear Father' would have to go. He wrote instead GREATLY REGRET TO INFORM YOU, crossed it out, and put HAVE MUCH PLEASURE IN INFORMING YOU. He scratched his head with his pencil. He felt he should send something snappy like UNCLE EXHONGKONG INFLEW LONDON SEEMS OK CASHWISE STATUSWISE LEGALWISE WISEWISE, but gave it up. A mind trained for the Oxford honour schools was too delicate an instrument for reducing to blunt cablese the ideas at that moment churning inside him.

It was eight in the morning after Lord Brickwood's arrival, which Teddy had to admit made a pretty agreeable day of it. Leaving the Trafalgar Club after lunch Uncle Horatio had announced, 'Now, my boy, I must go to the bank. Pott's, of course.'

Pott's in St James's Square was designed on the same lines as the Trafalgar Club, not being one of those vulgar sort of banks where you and I furtively slip across our cheques next to the local fishmonger dropping in the week's takings. At Pott's they handled some of the highest-classed overdrafts in the country, and gave the impression that lolly was, after all, a boring necessity like one's toothbrush or umbrella.

'I wish to speak to the manager,' Uncle Horatio announced at once, stepping up to the mahogany counter.

'What name?' demanded the severe bird in a stiff collar, ploughing his way through a pile of fivers.

'Lord Brickwood.'

'Oh, of course, my Lord.'

He pushed the fivers hastily aside, eager to be at his service. That's another odd thing—in these days when democracy is spread through the country like detergents, there's nothing like a title to make everyone perk up and take notice. I suppose when you can buy pretty well everything else on the h.p. it's got a priceless sort of standing, like a good golf handicap.

'I'm afraid the manager is at the Treasury at the moment, my Lord,' explained the bank clerk. 'Would one of the assistant managers do?'

'The senior one.'

'Naturally, my Lord. This way, if you please.'

Teddy and Uncle Horatio were shown into a gloomy room with a ten-square-foot desk, behind which a youngish fellow in striped trousers sat under a billiard-table lamp.

'I should like to open an account,' Uncle Horatio announced, when the pally stuff was over. 'I have only today returned to London after several years in business out East. I was not, alas, brought up to indulge in commerce, but these days a peer must cut his robes according to his cloth.'

As Teddy had gathered Uncle Horatio was pushing through deals since he tried to flog his pram in Kensington Gardens, he decided the old boy was being decently modest.

'Funds—considerable funds—will be shortly transferred from Hong Kong,' Lord Brickwood went on. 'This letter will be adequate reference, I'm sure—' He paused, adjusting his monocle. 'Were you—er, in financial circles during the War?'

'I was just old enough to do the whole time overseas in the Air Force,' smiled the manager.

'Oh, jolly good. I have many close friends among the Air Marshals. As I said, this letter will establish my bona fides and so on. I should like to open an account with some token figure—say a hundred pounds.' He produced a few notes from his wallet. 'If you could issue me with a cheque book—'

'But of course, Lord Brickwood.'

The banker pressed a bell.

'And now,' announced Uncle Horatio, fondly patting his breast pocket outside with Teddy on the steps, 'I must do a little shopping. First I must find a decent tailor and shirtmaker—I don't think I shall take my custom to the former ones, they were terribly old-fashioned even then—and afterwards I shall take enormous pleasure in buying you a wedding present.'

'No really,' exclaimed Teddy, rather alarmed. An uncle from Hong Kong might be pretty peeved at the non-appearance of your fiancée, but he'd be furious if he'd invested a silver chafing-dish or whatever in her as well. 'I mean, there's no rush. I'm sure she'll turn up all right in a day or two.' he added quickly. 'From the country, that is. But if she should decide to take a prolonged holiday—'

'Nonsense! We'll buy it this very afternoon. Then if your bride-to-be dislikes it there'll be time to have it changed.'

'I wouldn't want you to run short of ready cash—'

'My dear good boy! That doesn't enter into it. We shall open accounts everywhere. Taxi!'

Any doubts Teddy had about his uncle being stuffed to the eyeballs with rhino were washed away by the spending wave which lapped up and down Bond Street. Lord Brickwood re-equipped himself for life in the Old Country with a variety of implements from electric cigar cutters to fully furnished picnic baskets for fifteen people, not to mention several dozen silk ties, a couple of shooting sticks, and a five years' subscription to *Punch*. Teddy was so dazzled with the outlay he hardly noticed himself being presented with an all-electric kitchen, but he felt he could always ship it back later as it was only being put on his uncle's account.

Their last call was the Ritz.

'I've had all my correspondence and cables directed there,' Lord Brickwood explained as they reached the swing doors. 'I shall be very disappointed if they are unable to accommodate me. I have always held it the only hotel in London one can possibly stay in.'

'Uncle—' began Teddy.

A brilliant but simple idea burst in his mind. An uncle who obviously held the gorgeous East in fee should not only respond to a bit of spadework and save the fortunes of Brickwood and Vole, but shell out the lolly for a satirical night-club on the side. Then he and Abigail could walk down the aisle to the sound of joyous bells rather than the sordid ring of cash registers.

'Uncle,' he invited, 'unless you're particularly stuck on the Ritz, why don't you put up in the flat? I mean, there's bags of room, and you could spend as long as you liked in the bath and so on. As for the grub—'

'My dear boy.' Lord Brickwood laid a hand on Teddy's shoulder. He was delighted to notice his uncle so deeply touched. 'If I have learned any lesson from my long and eventful life, it is simply this—that the Ritz is no substitute for the home, however humble. I should be charmed to accept your most considerate offer. My effects, at present in the left luggage office at

Waterloo Station, are slight. Air travel, you know. All my heavy luggage is following by ship.'

'You're meaning to stay some time in London?' Teddy added hopefully.

'I intend,' explained Lord Brickwood solemnly, slipping his arm through his nephew's, 'to bathe it in the glow of my sunset years.'

He hailed a taxi for Eaton Square.

Lord Brickwood insisted on standing Teddy dinner at a small and smelly restaurant in Bayswater, on what struck the lad as the odd recommendation of its having once provided him with a banana during the War. After a few more stories about Poles his uncle had decided on an early night of it, and now appeared from his bedroom in the penthouse with shining morning face, wearing a bright blue silk dressing-gown decorated with white dragons.

'Good morning, my boy,' Uncle Horatio exclaimed as Teddy slipped the cable under the blotter. 'A capital night's sleep. Particularly considering this ghastly adjustment to London time. And now—' He rubbed his hands. 'Where is breakfast laid?'

'Breakfast? Well it isn't laid,' Teddy explained. 'I sort of pick it up in the kitchen as I go along.'

'Be a good lad and tell the cook I'll have bacon and eggs and a little kidney.'

'I'm afraid we haven't any kidneys,' continued Teddy anxiously. 'As a matter of fact, we haven't any bacon and eggs for the moment, either. And I'm sorry to say we've only Mrs. Gamewell who messes about with a bucket and doesn't turn up till ten thirty.' He was alarmed to see a frown congeal on his uncle's broad forehead. 'I usually shake out a plate of Whispie Krispies,' he added lamely.

'Pity. I was rather looking forward to a decent English breakfast. However, I am *en famille*, I suppose. What on earth did you say those peculiar things were called?'

Uncle Horatio ate his Whispie Krispies reading *The Times*, spending a good deal of attention on the Personal column.

'Dear old England!' he laughed, seeming to recover his good humour with the first of Mr. Brickwood's cigars. 'Hasn't changed a bit. Have you ever thought, Teddy, that whatever you want to do in this country somebody's formed a society against it? Blood sports, vivisection, fluoridization of water, being cremated, Sunday opening of pubs. There's a fortune to be made from it somewhere,' he added obscurely. 'Now—what are your plans for the morning?'

'I've got to slip round to the post office and a few places.'

'I'll just sit about here and make a few phone calls. Perhaps you have a copy of *Who's Who* handy? Excellent. I'll browse through the pages.

59

Such a useful publication for picking up one's old contacts. You might buy the *Financial Times* and *Country Life* for me somewhere, there's a good lad.'

Teddy dispatched his cable from the post office in Knightsbridge and crossed into Hyde Park. The place was bursting at the seams with spring, but he didn't notice the tulips or the rather jolly rabbits in the Dell or the boats splashing about the Serpentine or the couples risking a nasty attack of rheumatism by getting at it early on the damp grass. There is something about London parks conducive to thought, and Teddy strode beside Rotten Row falling heavily into meditation. He wondered anxiously if the plan for the reunion in bliss had somehow got stuck in the works. It was hard enough on a chap, he reflected, trying to get his fiancée back for his own benefit, let alone for his uncle's. If George had failed to do his stuff, he decided he would have to go round to Berkeley Square and grovel as elegantly as possible. He wanted to ring George up, but the establishment where the fellow had taken temporary residence in Notting Hill didn't run to a telephone. It suddenly struck Teddy he was half-way to Notting Hill anyway, and he decided to march on across Kensington Gardens to pay a call.

'Oo, Mr. Churchyard?' asked the woman with the mop on the front steps. 'What you mean him with the beard? The law came for him last Friday.'

'No, he's a sort of fair-haired chap with a chin,' Teddy described his friend. 'He tends to wear ties with little kangaroos on.'

'Oh, him with the late hours. He's gorn.'

'Gorn?'

She nodded. 'Gorn this morning. With a lady.'

'A lady?'

'Yes. He came back with her in his old boneshaker to pick up his things.'

'What sort of a lady?' asked Teddy narrowly.

'Search me, luv. You gets all sorts these days, dontcher?'

'Thank you,' nodded Teddy, leaving her to her mop.

Odd, he thought darkly. He stuck his hands deep in his pockets. George and Abigail? Surely not! But, he recalled bleakly, the pair of them became pretty pally those times she'd come up to Oxford. Then there was the incident of the umbrella. It hadn't been a very big umbrella, certainly. But there was more room for two under it than *that*.

'Impossible,' Teddy muttered.

He hailed a cab, and went round to Berkeley Square via Constance Spry.

'Oh, hello, Sydenham,' he greeted the chap in striped pants who opened the front door.

Butlers are far from extinct in the plushier London homes. The only difference these days

61

is they're all down on some company's wages books as catering supervisors.

'Why, it's Mr. Brickwood,' Sydenham greeted him. 'Good morning, sir.'

'I'd like to see Miss Abigail, please.'

'I'm afraid Miss Abigail's gone, sir.'

'Gone?'

'To an undisclosed destination, sir.'

'But dammit!' returned Teddy shortly. 'Surely you can disclose it to me?'

'I'm afraid it must be particularly undisclosed to you, sir,' the butler told him sombrely.

'Oh,' said Teddy. 'I see.' He paused. 'Thank you, Sydenham.'

Teddy strode into Berkeley Square. He found another bench. He sat down, and pretty stupid he felt, particularly holding all that mimosa. He suddenly uttered a cry. He'd remembered the episode of the strawberry ice. He bet that beastly man George wasn't really wiping it off her dress with his face-flannel as he came in. George always was one for the girls, Teddy reflected blackly, with a fine line of chat about romantic trips to the Pacific Isles, or if more convenient somewhere on the south coast.

'Blast him,' Teddy muttered, grinding his teeth so hard he pretty near chipped the enamel.

Stupid, you'll admit. But look at that paranoid idiot Othello, barging and booming all over the place and suffocating people, when the youngest school treat at the back of the stalls could tell him that handkerchief business was strictly on the level.

'He's not going to get away with that,' Teddy muttered fiercely.

He rose and started firmly back to the penthouse, pausing only to hand the mimosa with his compliments to a chap writing out parking tickets on the kerb.

CHAPTER NINE

'Hello!' Teddy exclaimed, as the lift doors slid apart downstairs at Eaton Square and Mrs. Gamewell stalked out. 'Finished early for the day?'

'I want my cards,' announced Mrs. Gamewell.

'Your cards? Good lord, what's up? I mean, you've been doing for us now almost as long as I can remember.'

'A fine way to treat me, I must say,' she continued, with the air of a prima donna just hissed off the stage at Covent Garden. 'My husband will have something to say, believe you me.'

'Oh, the gentleman in the flat is perfectly all right,' Teddy remembered. 'He's my Uncle Horatio, from Hong Kong.'

'Hong Kong! Colney Hatch, more likely. It's a

madhouse up there. A madhouse!' she emphasized, making for the front door. 'You'll hear more about this, mark my words.'

She left Teddy pretty baffled. He stepped into the lift and went up.

Despite his tortured soul, he'd become sharply aware on the way home of the now greater importance of buttering up uncle. He would clearly have to get the chap in a cracking mood before mentioning the London end of the family were as broke as British Railways and his fiancée had eloped with his best friend. He decided to bottle things up for a day or two, which would give Uncle Horatio time to attune himself to the London air, and all those considerable funds to come across from Hong Kong. Meanwhile, he felt the old boy hadn't really enjoyed his breakfast, even if he did get the portion of Whispie Krispies with the little plastic space-rocket in it. Teddy had outlined for himself vague menus of bangers and baked beans, but feeling he should provide something more recherché for lunch had stopped in Sloane Square and bought a tin of anchovies and a rather niffy Camembert.

'Oh, I'm sorry,' Teddy exclaimed, as the penthouse door opened. He seemed to have got the wrong flat again.

'Yais?' fluted a delicate-looking fellow with ginger sidewhiskers and a striped waistcoat.

'I—I was looking for Mr. Brickwood's place.'

The ginger fellow eyed Teddy as though he were the lad calling for the empties.

'Your name?'

'Mr. Brickwood. Edward Brickwood.'

'One moment. I will see if his Lordship is available.'

Teddy stood on the mat feeling pretty foolish, particularly, of course, with that Camembert.

'Lord Brickwood will see you now,' conceded the butler, sidling back.

Teddy went in, to find his uncle face down on the sofa eating a plover's egg and wearing only a bathtowel, with a young woman in a white overall massaging his back and another in a pink overall manicuring his nails.

'Teddy, my dear fellow! I was expecting you much sooner. What on earth can you have found in London to divert you at this hour of the day?'

'I—I didn't know you had company, Uncle,' he stammered.

'Sylvia and Hermione,' he introduced his attendants, peeling another egg. 'One does so miss one's Chinese massage. Yes, Alastair?' he asked, as the butler minced in.

'Some lovely provisions have arrived from Fortnum and Mason, sir.'

'Quick work,' nodded Lord Brickwood, as the girl in the white overall fondled his sacrospinalis. 'You've told the kitchen staff to go ahead, I hope? Good.'

'You've got quite darling cuticles,' murmured

the manicurist.

'Uncle—' Teddy burst out.

'Yes, my boy? I say, what on earth have you got in your hand?'

'It's a Camembert.'

'Do take it out to the kitchen, Alastair.'

'Yes, indeed, sir.'

'There's these too.' Teddy pulled out his anchovies as the butler removed the cheese at an arm's length. 'Did you bring all these people from Hong Kong with you?' he asked anxiously.

'Oh, dear me, no. That's *just* the spot, Hermione, between the shoulder blades. I felt this morning, my boy, that your *ménage*, though perfectly adequate for a young gentleman of enviably simple tastes like yourself, was hardly adequate to one, alas, wedded lovingly to his creature comforts. So I rang one of those excellent agency places. I asked them, however, to keep the staff down to a bare minimum of ten.'

'Ten!'

'Yes, you'd be surprised how quickly they're used up. There's a butler, footman, three in the kitchen, these two charming young ladies, chauffeur—'

'But we haven't got a car!' exclaimed Teddy.

'Good lord, you don't mean to say your father moves round London in a common omnibus? I will ring up that place in Piccadilly and ask them to send round a Rolls. Yes, Alastair?'

'A Miss Turnpenny, my Lord.'

'Who on earth could she be?' frowned Uncle Horatio. 'Young? Old? Ugly? Attractive? Collecting for the lifeboats? Flat next door, come to borrow a cup of sugar?'

'She has a tiny little typewriter and an absolutely huge note-book, my Lord.'

'Oh, my secretary. So speedily efficient, that agency. Do show her in.'

A pretty little girl of about nineteen appeared, with her hair in the absolutely bang-on fashion, just like all the other little nineteen-year-old girls in London. She was probably surprised to find her employer half-naked under the ministrations of Hermione and Sylvia, but she had one of those faces which did not readily express powerful emotion. In fact, she had one of those faces which did not readily express anything.

'Do drop your typewriter, my dear,' invited Lord Brickwood, wrapping the towel round him and sitting up as Hermione came to the end of her repertoire. 'What's your full name, now?'

'Dawn Turnpenny,' the secretary returned flatly.

'Dawn! How delightful! And where do you come from, Dawn?'

'Petts Wood.'

'Naturally, you do!' chortled Uncle Horatio. 'I am not very clear where Petts Wood happens to be, but I can so easily imagine it. Emerald

67

glades, people with such delightful pets as yourself sporting in the shafts of golden sunlight.'

'It's on the Southern electric,' Dawn explained.

'Ah, my illusions are shattered these days as regularly as household teacups. I have some letters and so on to dictate this afternoon, Dawn. Meanwhile this young gentleman will look after you.' He indicated Teddy with a nod. 'Would it be a bore changing into a decent suit, my boy?' he asked. 'We have a lady coming to lunch.'

'Oh, have we?' Teddy returned.

'A Mrs. Prothero, now living in Edinburgh. Perfectly charming. She is flying down, as we have a little business to discuss. I do hate conducting such matters in public restaurants with waiters listening behind all the pillars. Particularly with such a sensitive soul as Mrs. Prothero, who is quite uncontaminated with the sordid brush of commerce. The same time tomorrow, girls,' he announced as the pair folded their overalls and prepared to go. 'Our guest should be here in twenty minutes. Alastair!' he called.

'My Lord?'

'Put the champagne on the ice,' commanded Uncle Horatio.

He made for his dressing-room, humming a few bars of *Into Battle*.

CHAPTER TEN

'It will be quite an intimate little luncheon,' Uncle Horatio explained to Teddy, watching the pretty girl in a frilly apron arranging the table. 'Just the three of us. I am looking forward to it tremendously. Ah, the flowers I see, Alastair,' he broke off, as the butler appeared behind a load of cellophane boxes. 'I always think orchids go so well with cutlery, don't you, Teddy?'

'I say, Uncle—' began Teddy awkwardly, standing by the fireplace in his best suit. Glancing round, he felt that what with the flowers and the previous day's purchases and all the people, the penthouse was running into the overcrowded tenement category. 'Uncle, I'm sure you don't really want me hanging about, do you? I mean, if you and Mrs. Prothero are planning a cosy little chat, I'd be quite happy to clear off for a sandwich at the Antelope.'

'My dear boy!' Lord Brickwood threw a shocked glance through his monocle. 'Surely you would never expect me to turn one of the family away from my table? And furthermore, Teddy, no gentleman ever lunches on sandwiches. If you find some of the conversation a little over your head, I know I can rely on you to sit there quietly and make perfectly charming remarks at appropriate intervals. You will find Grace Prothero an absolutely delightful person. Yes, my dear?' he broke off, as Dawn appeared. 'Ah, the menu.' He inspected the typed card thoughtfully. 'Caviar, *consommé*, salmon mousse, chicken ... all easily digestible and suitable for an informal midday meal in warm weather. My dear Dawn, do you like working here?'

'Can't say as I've worked here much yet.'

'Well, do you think that you're *going* to like it?' beamed Lord Brickwood encouragingly.

'Can't say.'

'I am delighted to find such caution in a pretty young girl like yourself.'

'Ow, go on,' said Dawn, simpering a bit.

'I shall have lots for you to do this afternoon, Dawn. You are in no hurry, I take it, to rush back to the bewitching boskiness of Petts Wood? Excellent. Mrs. Prothero,' Uncle Horatio went on to Teddy, 'is the widow of some quite excellent industrialist on Clydeside. I was fortunate enough to make her acquaintance in the bar of the Peninsula Hotel in Hong Kong, when she was passing through on a world tour to soothe the grief of her dear husband's unfortunate demise. It will be so delightful to recall old times. Our business matters can be dismissed in a few minutes.'

'My Lord,' announced Alastair, appearing in the doorway. 'Mrs. Grace Prothero.'

'My dear, dear Gracie,' glowed Uncle

Horatio, fair skipping across the carpet to grasp the hand of a middle-aged dark-haired lady with the comfortably elegant appearance of a well-preserved Edwardian sofa. 'It seems but yesterday—'

'And friend,' added Alastair.

Lord Brickwood paused in the action of sweeping the mixture of fingers and well-set diamonds towards his lips. He eyed a little man in a plain blue suit, with a red face and hair like the bristles of a brand-new scrubbing-brush.

'Mr. Angus McInch,' Alastair clarified matters.

'Writer to the Signet,' added Mr. McInch, offering a bony hand with an air that indicated he most certainly wanted it back.

'My attorney,' Mrs. Prothero cooed in explanation. 'As we are discussing business, Horatio, I'm sure you wouldn't object?'

'No, no, not at all,' replied Lord Brickwood blankly. He screwed in his monocle and eyed the Scot as though he were one of the less publicized ingredients of haggis. 'I am of course perfectly delighted ... perfectly ... there is quite enough caviar to do four, I'm sure.'

'Air—'m no' a great eater,' put in Mr. McInch.

'I am sure the presence of Mr. McInch will greatly expedite—indeed, simplify—our task,' went on Lord Brickwood, recovering himself. 'My kinsman, Edward,' he added, introducing

71

Teddy.

'Wheel,' observed Mr. McInch, after a quick session of introductions and reminiscences. 'Is ye partner no' here, ye Ludship?'

'Ah, my partner.' Lord Brickwood twirled his monocle on the cord. 'No, I'm afraid he has been delayed.'

'Air—delayed?'

'Yes, delayed,' repeated Lord Brickwood, a shade impatiently. 'Unavoidably.'

'And where would that unfortunate unavoidability be?'

'His estates in the West Country, you know. Frightfully busy this time of the year. Lambing and calving, hedging and ditching, and so on.'

'Wheel, I'd verra much like to make his acquaintance. After all, I gather he represents half the security of the new venture?'

'Cigarette?' asked Lord Brickwood.

'Och, no. I dinna smoke.'

'Glass of champagne?'

'I'm a lifelong teetotaller.'

'How's the old complaint?'

'Complaint? I ha' no' had a day's illness in my life.'

'It's getting rather warm in here,' announced Lord Brickwood. 'Alastair, open a window.'

'Now, let's not have one single word of business until we've enjoyed this absolutely wonderful lunch,' smiled Mrs. Prothero, sipping her champagne. 'After all, Horatio,

72

there's a time and place for everything.'

'How I agree with you, my dear,' added Lord Brickwood, patting the diamonds warmly. 'Let us not cloy the hungry edge of appetite with sordid commerce. Alastair, take Mr. McInch's briefcase. Perhaps he would care for a small glass of ginger-pop?'

Teddy didn't enjoy his lunch more than the meal with his father the day he was sent down from Oxford. The caviar stuff he'd heard a good deal about, but it was jolly salty and you had to keep chasing it over your plate like ball bearings. The *consommé* and mucked-up salmon were all right, but he felt everything would have slipped down more easily if there hadn't been something of an atmosphere round the table. Mrs. Prothero was in fine form prattling away about Kowloon and chopsticks, but Mr. McInch sat there with the air of John Knox at the Windmill. Even Lord Brickwood's ebullience seemed to have turned flat, for though he glowed spasmodically in Mrs. Prothero's direction and patted the diamonds pretty freely between courses, he seemed to keep slipping into great troughs of silent thought.

As Uncle Horatio was swirling his brandy meditatively round the snifter, Mr. McInch remarked, 'Air.'

They turned towards him.

'Air—would ye ha' the address of ye partner's

estate on you?' he asked. 'As ye'll appreciate, it's verra important—'

'He has several estates,' Lord Brickwood explained briefly. 'Shooting-boxes, fishing-lodges, castles, and so on. But that is all of purely academic importance. I have been keeping from you a little secret.'

Everyone looked interested.

'No gentleman ever discloses secrets before luncheon,' he went on genially. 'Don't you agree, my dear? It is simply this. My partner has transferred his interest.'

'Wheel—' said Mr. McInch, looking like John Knox at the Windmill feeling interested in spite of himself. 'And to whom, may I ask?'

'To the young gentleman sitting opposite.'

Teddy sat up.

'To him?' exclaimed Mrs. Prothero, a slight frown falling on her features like someone's indentation on an Edwardian sofa.

'Air—'

'Yes. To my nephew Edward Brickwood. An excellent young man who'—Lord Brickwood reached for a cigar—'is very shortly to be married to Abigail, the only daughter of Mr. Charles Fitzhammond.'

'But of course!' Mrs. Prothero's face sprang back to shape. 'I noticed it in the papers.'

'Wheel—'

'An excellent match, we all feel in the family.'

'Aye, it puts a somewhat different complexion

on the matter.'

'Exactly. I'm sure we needn't discuss the transaction any further. If you will prepare the necessary documents, Mr. McInch, Mrs. Prothero and myself will sign them.'

Teddy scratched his head. His mind, as usual when finding itself at a loose end, had been performing a scene or two of his play, and it could afford to lash out a bit on the cast. As Sirs John Gielgud and Michael Redgrave had just finished a snappy exchange with Vivien Leigh to loud applause Teddy hadn't followed the argument round the table, but he fancied there was a flaw in it somewhere.

'Air,' announced Mr. McInch. 'I'd like a word or two alone with young Mr. Brickwood.'

'My dear sir!' exclaimed Lord Brickwood. 'Surely you don't doubt for one moment his bona fides? Really, Gracie! In my family we are used to discussing matters like gentlemen.'

'I hae only one or two wee points, yer Ludship.'

'I suppose Mr. McInch *is* my attorney,' conceded Mrs. Prothero, twisting the stem of her *crème de menthe* reflectively.

'Of course, I have really not the slightest objection,' declared Lord Brickwood, glancing round the table rapidly. 'If you will just excuse us one moment,' he went on, rising, 'I shall be able to furnish the young man with the necessary material from my files. Come,

75

Teddy.'

'Uncle,' began Teddy anxiously, as they disappeared into his Lordship's bedroom, 'I think I had better explain here and now that in fact I'm not—'

'For God's sake shut up,' hissed Uncle Horatio, gathering an armful of papers. 'Be a good boy, now, and take these outside and keep that ghastly bit of ground bait for the Loch Ness Monster quiet for ten minutes.'

'But Uncle! I really must tell you that as far as Abigail—'

'Whatever he asks, just say your lips are sealed.'

'Uncle! I've simply got to let you know—'

Lord Brickwood stamped his foot. 'Really, boy, do stop blathering. You've only got to put up with the man for ten minutes. All right, five minutes, if you like. You can always pretend you're looking for something in the documents, dammit.

'I'm only trying to say that I'm afraid we're misleading Mr. McInch—'

'Misleading?' Lord Brickwood glared through his monocle. 'You are not suggesting, I hope, that your own uncle is doing anything in the slightest shady?'

'No, of course not, but—'

'Now do pipe down, Teddy, and get on with it. Surely you can see I'm merely trying to satisfy some small-minded pernickety Scot, who probably counts his small change every night and puts buttons in the collection? Here we are,' he announced jovially, propelling Teddy into the dining-room. 'I have instructed my nephew to discuss anything you wish with the utmost frankness, Mr. McInch. Mrs. Prothero and myself will retire to the drawing-room next door. Come, Gracie,' he ended, offering his arm. 'The view of Battersea Power Station is quite remarkable.'

He left Teddy with a pile of papers a couple of inches thick, facing Mr. McInch over the remains of the dessert.

'Air,' observed Mr. McInch.

'Another cup of coffee?' asked Teddy.

'I dinna drink more than one.' He gave Teddy a glance as prickly as a field of thistles. 'To business,' he went on, opening his briefcase. 'How many of these pagodas are ye proposing to build?'

Teddy stared at him. What he really wanted to say was, 'Look here, McInch, I'm sure you're really a very decent sort, and jolly conscientious ferreting round the old torts and hereditaments and advowsons and so on, and believe me I'm absolutely bursting to help you in your present onerous task, but unfortunately I happen to know sweet Fanny Adams about it.'

But he paused. Businessmen, he felt, moved in mysterious ways, particularly one with such broad ideas as Uncle Horatio. There must be some jolly hard-headed reason, Teddy felt, for his uncle suddenly installing him in the merchant venture as his partner. Besides, once Uncle had collected a packet with these pagodas, whatever they were, he would be even more inclined to dip in the pocket for the benefit of Brickwood and Vole, followed smartly in the queue by the new satirical nightclub. He decided that whatever Uncle Horatio suggested, he deserved to be backed as closely as the gum on a threepenny stamp.

'I was asking you a question,' said Mr. McInch, in a voice suggesting that Bannockburn had just come to mind.

'I must consult the relevant documents,' muttered Teddy, hurriedly turning over the pages.

He had to confess they weren't of enormous help. The first was headed HARRY'S FORM BULLETIN, and went on to discuss the chances for the Spring Meeting at Newmarket. Underneath was a laundry bill written half in Chinese. Next came a brief letter from some solicitors in Hong Kong, saying mysteriously, 'Dear Sir, You really cannot expect us to advise that you will not encounter the difficulties you mention on arrival at London Airport, in view of the circumstances of your original departure from the United Kingdom.' The rest was the manuscript of a six-hundred-page American novel about the sex life of the inhabitants of a Tennessee tobacco farm, which Lord Brickwood had taken to read in bed. He frowned.

'Wheel?' demanded Mr. McInch impatiently.

'My lips are sealed,' announced Teddy, piling the papers together again.

'I dinna get your meaning, Mr. Brickwood.'

Teddy shrugged his shoulders. 'Sealed,' he repeated vaguely.

Mr. McInch bristled like a terrier spotting the postman. 'P'raps, Mr. Brickwood, ye will allow me to refresh your memory? The company in which my client is to invest a very considerable sum of money was formed by his Ludship to erect holiday pagodas for American tourists in Hong Kong. Correct?'

'Of course,' nodded Teddy.

'Wheel, noo. I should like to know how many pagodas there are to be. Not that I myself,' added Mr. McInch, 'would think much of taking me own holidays in a pagoda.'

'I think I'd better consult the relevant documents,' repeated Teddy quickly.

'I can save you a wee bit of trouble, Mr. Brickwood. I hae the suspicion the figures do not exist.'

'Really?' asked Teddy, interested.

'Mr. Brickwood, I should be obliged if ye'd be frank with me.'

'My lips are sealed,' Teddy pointed out.

'In which case I hae no alternative than to go

at once to the polis.'

'To the which?'

'The polis. Scotland Yard.'

'Here, I say,' exclaimed Teddy crossly. 'What an utterly beastly suggestion! If you've got the absolute neck to come in here and gorge on my uncle's grub and then sit back and infer that he's nothing but a common—'

'I hae my duty as an attorney and a citizen.'

'I'm not at all certain you don't deserve a jolly good punch on the—'

'Aye. That would mean an action for personal damages.'

'Look here, Mr. McInch, it should be perfectly obvious to the merest dim-wit that my uncle is a man of very considerable—'

He was interrupted by the drawing-room door opening.

'Teddy! My boy!' exclaimed Lord Brickwood. 'You must be the very first to hear. I have some absolutely wonderful news.'

'Oh, yes?'

'Gracie and myself have just become engaged to be married.'

He advanced across the room, taking Mrs. Prothero by the hand as though leading her into the winner's paddock after the Grand National.

'Good lord,' murmured Teddy. His mouth, already open to emit an additional threat at Mr. McInch, widened further.

'I am quite the happiest woman in the whole

wide world!' contributed Mrs. Prothero, clasping her hands together.

'And I,' announced Lord Brickwood, 'am the luckiest man alive. Could I have dared to think so short a while ago in Hong Kong that Grace would become the sugar in my cup of happiness?'

'Dear Teddy!' exclaimed Mrs. Prothero, advancing on him. 'You must give me a great big kiss.'

'In the future Lady Brickwood,' observed Uncle Horatio, 'I have not only found a wife, but you, Teddy, have found an auntie.'

'Air,' remarked Mr. McInch. 'Wheel.'

'I do wish you'd stop making those disgusting noises,' complained Lord Brickwood shortly.

'Mrs. Prothero—I hae something of the utmost importance to say to you.'

'My dear McInch,' frowned Uncle Horatio, 'surely you must have some feelings beneath that exterior of Grampian granite? A moment such as this is totally unsuited for the intrusion of solicitors.'

'Mrs. Prothero, I hae to insist—'

'Really!' she chided the chap. 'You must see I have other things on my mind just now.'

'A matter of extreme urgency—'

'Damn it, McInch!' exploded Lord Brickwood. 'If you're so worried about getting your fiddling little bill paid—'

'I will nae be insulted any longer,' snapped

Mr. McInch, jumping up. 'If you wish to make a bloody fool of yourself, madam, I can only say my conscience is totally clear that you did it in flat contradiction to the advice of your attorney.'

'How *dare* you!' exclaimed Mrs. Prothero, going pink.

'Get out, you abominable little addled Scotch egg,' added Lord Brickwood, 'before I ask my nephew to break your blasted neck.'

'That will be quite unnecessary. I am taking my leave.' He picked up his briefcase. He gave Mrs. Prothero a hurt, crushed glance, like the spider if Bruce had trodden on the thing afterwards. 'You always know where you can find me,' he ended.

'Get out!' roared Lord Brickwood, raising his foot.

The door slammed. Uncle Horatio made a dive for the diamonds again. 'My dear, so utterly distressing! What a perfectly uncouth little man! He's unmarried, I suppose? H'm. I thought so. Jealous, of course.'

'Jealous, Horatio?'

Lord Brickwood nodded gravely. 'You'd be surprised what notions they harbour about their attractive lady clients, these solicitors. Expected to do pretty well out of it, too, I daresay. I am a man of the world. I see such things. Better have someone take a sharp look at your accounts, too. I've never seen a worse embezzlement face. You will be much better with your affairs in the hands of my own solicitors,' he went on, patting the diamonds. 'Duff and Trimm, a small firm down in Old Bailey. They've done a lot for me in the past. Alastair, another bottle of champagne!' he commanded. 'You must drink our health, Teddy. Then I'm afraid I must leave you to your own devices for the afternoon. Gracie and I have to slip down to Asprey's and choose the ring.'

CHAPTER ELEVEN

While Uncle Horatio was preparing to entertain in Eaton Square, George Churchyard was driving Morag in his old square-fronted MG along the Hog's Back, that straight stretch of road with one of the most delightful views in southern England, if only you had time from dodging destruction in the traffic to look at it.

'I know just the pub for a quick lunch the far side of Alton,' he said, turning his eyes to think how nicely her blond hair blew about in the wind.

'What was that, darling?' asked Morag, as he had been slipping neatly between a pair of converging lorries at the time.

'Not nervous, are you?' George laughed.

'Oh, no, darling. I'm sure you haven't lost a passenger yet.'

George put his foot down, overtaking a cycling club out nose-to-tail enjoying themselves. He felt everything was developing rather nicely. Apart from a fortnight of blazing sunshine, fabulous food, and attentive service by devoted stewards as promised in the advertisements, who knew? Some terrific West End impresario might well be aboard, resting from counting the nightly takings. Watching the peformance every night for a couple of weeks would surely bring the fellow to his knees with a contract. And then, of course, there was Morag.

A cloud appeared on the horizon.

There is a make of small car which slouches along our dear old British roads resembling a bad-tempered black beetle with its back up. The *marque* has such optional extras as stickers covering the rear window to recall ghastly English seaside resorts, a little red skeleton bobbing up and down and grinning at you, or a cat with luminous eyes, and a characteristic performance of proceeding up hill and down dale at exactly thirty miles an hour slap in the middle of the road. These cars are never, of course, driven by you or me. They are always in the charge of half-blind stone-deaf morons with all the windows shut. The one to whom George Churchyard was now announcing his presence by keeping his fist on the horn button appeared from behind as a squat ape-like figure in a bowler hat, crouched intently over the steering column as though waiting for the front wheels to drop off.

'Blithering idiot,' muttered George. A frown crossed his face, which usually had an expression of honest friendliness, like the chaps in the cigarette advertisements. 'Forgotten to put up his L plates,' he added, trying to overtake and retreating in the teeth of an oncoming Jaguar.

Among other vehicles which enjoy the lavish freedom of our highways are those weird agricultural implements, several yards wide, trundled behind tractors by farmers deeply absorbed in their agricultural problems. One of these now swung from a gap in the hedge ahead, allowing the beetle car to exhibit another of its features. They either run at thirty miles an hour or stop dead. This one stopped, and George ran into the back.

'Such *language*,' murmured Morag to herself, tidying her hair as George crossed to the beetle driver's window. 'Quite *Clinical*.'

'I am not in the least interested in these puerile outpourings,' announced the beetle driver, speaking for the first time as he climbed out.

George was slightly put off to find the chap somehow rather larger than his car. He had a pink face, sharp blue eyes, and the thickest and prickliest eyebrows George had ever encountered. These now rose slowly, reminding

85

him of a pair of hairy caterpillars crawling up a brick wall.

'Your total lack of manners is entirely your own misfortune,' continued the other driver. 'That you fail to look at the road ahead is everybody's else's.'

'You've smashed one of the headlights,' complained George furiously. 'I'm hurrying to get up to Southampton and you were crawling along at ten miles an hour—'

'I, too, am hurrying to get to Southampton, but am refraining from doing so at a pace designed to litter the highway with corpses.'

'Taking up the entire road—'

'Oh? You would oblige everyone else to drive in the gutter?'

'You stopped without the slightest warning—'

'Blast your boots man!' exclaimed the beetle driver. 'What the hell did you want me to do? Send you a ruddy postcard?'

'How the devil did you expect me to pull up in that distance?' demanded George hotly.

'By getting your bleeding brakes tightened, that's how.'

It's a sad reflection on modern life that nothing causes such idiotic arguments between sensible adults like motoring, unless it's matrimony. After a few personal observations both drivers finally shook their fists, slammed the doors, and started the engines.

'That bowler-hatted baboon should be locked up as a menace to society,' snorted George, trying to put as much of the Southampton road between the pair of them as possible.

'He's probably simply *writhing* inside with the most *unspeakable* repressions, darling,' suggested Morag charitably.

The pub past Alton was one of those old timbered inns with all the rooms at different levels, which over the years have grown pleasantly into the English landscape. The pair's entrance made quite a stir in the bar parlour, what with Morag now wearing a yellow silk shift, a white rope, and gold sandals.

'After the foaming tankard how about the groaning board, as they say in the tourist advertisements?' announced George, quickly finishing his pint. 'I'm famished.'

'I've positive pangs,' agreed Morag.

They went into the little empty stone flagged dining-room. They sat down comfortably and picked up the menu. The door opened, and the beetle driver strode in.

The two men glared. It is really rather unfair if you have an argument with somebody on the road to meet them again over lunch. But I suppose if it happened more often there'd be hardly any accidents at all. Morag took a mirror from her raffia handbag and started inspecting her face. The waitress with the spotty apron and sinusitis invited them to order now.

'Roast beef,' announced George.

'Yes, I'm an utter carnivore,' concurred Morag.

'Roast beef,' growled the beetle driver, clearly regarding it as a poor alternative to George's head on a salver.

He opened the *Daily Telegraph* and disappeared behind it.

'I wish I was more of an expert about life on the ocean wave,' remarked George, breaking a silence as brittle as a bar of butterscotch. 'I've always flown about the world before.'

'But darling, I know as much about ships as I do about coal-mining.'

'How did you get the job?'

'It was at one of my parties. I don't know, quite. I don't think Fabian does either.'

'But supposing you're seasick?' asked George with concern.

'I'm absolutely bound to be, darling. I can't walk down Bond Street past Gieves' window without feeling definitely queasy.'

There was a rustle of the *Telegraph*. 'Waitress! Water.'

'Do you suppose we'll have to sit at the Captain's table?' George went on.

'I'm sure that would be perfectly bestial.'

'Yes, these old salts are shocking bores,' George nodded. 'Nothing to talk about except some terribly uninteresting typhoon they weathered in the Sargasso Sea, or whatever.'

The *Telegraph* flashed down. 'I should be very much obliged, sir, if you would kindly refrain from making insulting remarks about the British Merchant Marine.'

'And I should be very much obliged,' George returned evenly, 'if you would kindly refrain from butting into our conversation.'

'I happen,' declared the man, his eyebrows working like a pair of battling stoats, 'to be descended from a very old seafaring family.'

'Well, my dear, we're all out of the Ark,' murmured Morag.

George laughed.

'My grandfather,' barked the beetle driver, 'was sunk at Jutland. My great-grandfather was wrecked off the Cape in his own tea clipper. One of my remoter ancestors, I might tell you, was run aground by the Spanish Armada.'

'Gallant sailors all, I'm sure,' George conceded generously.

'If rather accident-prone,' added Morag throatily.

Further conversation was fortunately forestalled by the appearance of the sinusoidal girl with the beef.

'Waitress!' called the pink-faced man.

'Yers?'

'You call this roast beef?'

'That's what it says on the menu,' she pointed out, sniffing.

'I will admit it. I will even admit the material

you have placed in front of me is of bovine origin. I am merely remarking that you have somehow managed to change it beyond recognition.'

'It's no good talking to me.' She gave another sniff. 'I didn't cook it, I'm sure.'

'Roast beef, may I point out for your edification, should be red, juicy, and oozing blood in the middle. This is grey, desiccated, and covered with gravy apparently made from brown boot-polish.'

'Nobody else has complained,' ended the waitress, regarding this as clinching the argument.

'I can't stand people who make a fuss in restaurants,' generalized George loudly in Morag's direction.

'If there were more people with the courage to speak out, damn you, the public would have less sludge thrown at them by a bunch of bone-idle profiteering caterers.'

'I do wish you wouldn't keep interrupting our conversation,' added George wearily.

The man rose.

'I don't want any lunch.'

'You'll have to pay, all the same,' declared the waitress.

'You may bring me the bill in the bar. And kindly inform the management that I am perfectly agreeable to pay good money for the privilege of not eating in their establishment.

Good morning.'

The door slammed.

'Thank the lord we won't have to set eyes on that one again,' remarked George. 'More Yorkshire?'

CHAPTER TWELVE

The *Snowdonia* was one of those absolutely up-to-the-minute liners in which everything seems to be made of plastic, including the sea. She didn't look anything like a ship, of course. They never do these days. It's sad that such jolly concomitants of maritime life as funnels and masts, the smell of tar, and the whistle of wind in the rigging have been banished as firmly as keelhauling and walking the plank. The *Snowdonia* was a great white slim thing, not beautiful but elegant. In the middle of all the crates and cranes of Southampton Docks she reminded you of those skinny models they keep photographing against old brick walls and empty milk-bottles for the fashion magazines.

But even if a ship resembles a floating soap-dish, she can't sail without a captain.

It's on odd thing, but in a world where kings have hung up their crowns wholesale, generals have tossed aside their swords and scarlet, millionaires stampede to scatter their millions on deserving causes, and the great Ministers of State burst their waistcoat buttons on the telly proving they're just homely fellows like you and me, only one figure is left swaddled in magnificence.

The ship's captain.

Dictators sit quaking in bullet-proof hideouts thinking of other would-be dictators, chairmen wake screaming in the night from dreams about shop stewards, judges blanch to the roots of their wigs at backhanders in Latin from higher courts, the governors of jails and even the headmasters of English public schools daren't treat the inmates exactly how they'd like. But a ship's captain at sea can't be disobeyed or chucked out or, on some mornings, even mildly contradicted. He is the only representative for hundreds of miles in all directions of both the Queen and God.

And Captain Alfred Kettlehorn looked like it.

'Steward!' He stormed into his day cabin, almost hitting a little man with the air of a tippling jockey as he chucked aside his bowler. 'Who the devil are you?'

'Huffkins, sir. Your new steward.'

'What happened to the feller who looked after me last trip?'

'It is said in the stewards' mess, sir, that he has entered some sort of home.'

'H'm. Where's me uniform?'

'Laid out in your night cabin, sir.'

'Compliments to the Staff Captain, and I want to see him as convenient. What's this? Supernumerary crew?' Captain Kettlehorn scowled at a letter on his desk. 'Get him up to my cabin, quick.'

'Very good, sir.'

Five minutes later Captain Kettlehorn emerged, dressed overall. There was a knock at the door.

'Enter!'

George Churchyard stepped in.

The poor chap had been having a confusing hour of it.

'Ah, Jolly Jack,' he'd greeted the fat man in bell-bottoms at the top of the gangway, after Morag had disappeared for some last-minute shopping. 'Pins and things,' she'd announced vaguely. 'I'm sure I shall be absolutely *desperate* for pins.'

'Well, Jolly Jack,' George asked him. 'Where do I go?'

The Quartermaster regarded George warily, having an eye for the bearers of bills, summonses, maintenance orders, warrants and other inconveniences for the ship's company.

'Passenger embarkation six o'clock,' the Quartermaster announced.

'I'm not actually a passenger,' George explained. 'I suppose you'd say I was on the staff. Who's going to show me to my cabin? There's no need to be so rude,' he added, as the

93

Quartermaster told him.

'Down aft, you,' grunted the sailor, jerking his thumb.

George strode down the deck. If this was the sort of welcome you got aboard the Fitzhammond ships, he thought, he'd jolly well report the fellow to the Company.

'Here, I say!' He hailed a grey-haired man in gold braid hurrying towards him. 'Direct me to my cabin, will you?'

'First Class, sir?' asked the Purser, switching his mind from some complicated logistics concerning stuffed olives.

'Naturally.'

'Port or starboard, sir?'

'I really haven't the faintest idea.'

'Did you happen to remember your number on the plan, sir?' asked the Purser, turning on his professional smile.

'Nobody's bothered to tell me yet,' replied George, becoming a little bad-tempered.

'These office wallahs.' The Purser shook his head. 'I'm extremely sorry, sir. I assure you it was merely an oversight. If you'd care to step down to my office, sir, we could consult the passenger list?'

'That won't be the slightest use,' George told him briefly. 'Because I'm not a passenger. I happen to be Mr. Churchyard, the First Class entertainer.'

'Alf!' The Purser hailed a passing deck-hand.

'Take this geezer and show him where to sling his hammock.'

George finally found himself in a cabin the size of a Victorian wardrobe, marked BAND AND ORGANIST, with half a dozen bunks, no porthole, and the smell of a well-used seaside bathing-hut on a hot day.

'I'm damn well going to complain to the Captain,' he muttered to himself angrily.

At that moment a white-jacketed steward conveniently appeared with an invitation to call on exactly the same chap.

Stepping through the door of the day-cabin below the bridge, George was swept with the feeling he'd set eyes on this Captain fellow somewhere before. He took another look.

'Good lord!' A smile spread slowly over his face. This was something really rich. 'Why, you were the old—you were the chap in the car.' He gave a laugh. 'I hardly recognized you, all dressed up. That's a lesson for both of us, don't you think? We'd better let bygones be hasbeens, now we're both in the same—'

'Stand to attention when you're addressing the Master!' roared Captain Kettlehorn.

George laughed louder. 'Yes, I can see you're really the chauffeur of this jolly old lugger. Those remarks I made at lunch were, of course, entirely—'

'Stand to attention, blast your bleeding boots!'

Something in the Captain's face, which was thrust within two inches of his own with its eyebrows bristling like electrified hedgehogs, caused George's smile to curl up and die. He shifted into that compromise stance popular with theatregoers during the National Anthem.

'Name?' snapped Captain Kettlehorn.

'Churchyard.'

'I didn't ask what you looked like. I asked who you blasted well happened to be.'

'Churchyard's my name.'

'Sir! You address the Captain as "sir"!'

'It is admittedly a rather unusual name—sir—' George continued, wondering wildly if he could bring the conversation from this lunatic level. 'I believe I am descended from Thomas Churchyard, soldier and poet, born in the year fifteen—'

'I am not in the slightest interested in the details of your procreation, fascinating as they may be. Stand to attention!'

'Yes, of course—'

'Sir!'

'Sir.'

Captain Kettlehorn slowly withdrew his face. He silently settled himself in his armchair. He produced a Sherlock Holmes pipe, and blew through it loudly.

'Perhaps you would have the condescension to inform me,' he enquired quietly, filling it with tobacco that looked like Christmas pudding, 'exactly your duties aboard my ship?'

George licked his lips. He fancied he felt seasick.

'I'm the entertainer,' he explained. 'Sir.'

'What do you do? Sing? Play the banjo? Saw women in half? Eh?'

'I sort of tell funny stories,' George admitted lamely.

'Tell me one.'

'What, now?'

The Captain nodded. 'You said you were the entertainer. Right you are. Entertain me.'

'But I really need music and lights and—'

'I happen to be blessed with a particularly vivid imagination.'

George swallowed. He felt that someone had lined his throat with blotting-paper. 'This is a story about a Red Indian Chief,' he started nervously. 'He was a very rich and civilized Indian Chief, and he had three squaws. The Indian Chief himself slept in a big double bed,' George persisted, aware that in the past he had given crisper performances. 'But the three squaws followed the old tribal custom of sleeping on hides on the floor. The first squaw slept on a lion's hide, the second—'

A telephone rang.

'Captain. Yes? Umm...' There followed a five-minute conversation about the gyro compass. 'Proceed,' ordered Captain Kettlehorn, replacing the receiver.

'Perhaps you'd like me to start again from the beginning, sir?'

'Heaven forbid.'

'The first squaw slept on a lion's hide,' George continued doggedly, 'the second squaw slept on a zebra's hide, and the third squaw slept on a hippopotamus' hide. In the fullness of time the squaw who slept on the lion's hide produced a son. The Chief was naturally delighted at becoming the father of a brave—'

'Get on with it, man, get on with it. I haven't got all night.'

'No, of course not—'

'Sir!'

'Of course not, sir. Shortly afterwards, the squaw who slept on the zebra's hide also produced a son. And a little later the squaw who slept on the hippopotamus' hide produced twin sons,' George ended in a rush. 'Which proves that the squaw on the hippopotamus is equal to the sum of the squaws on the other two hides.'

'Proceed.'

'That's—that's all, sir.'

'The point, if I may say so, seems as elusive as the needle's in the haystack.'

'If you can recall the theorem of Pythagoras, sir—' tried George helpfully.

'Of course I can recall the theorem of Pythagoras. How the devil do you imagine I navigate my ship? Now look here, Mr. Graveyard, Churchyard, or whoever you are.'

The Captain rose. 'If the Company pays you to mouth such rubbish, that's their affair. I can only say I consider it nothing but an insult to everyone else on board who puts in an honest day's work. I don't want a squeak out of you for the rest of the trip. Understand? As far as I am concerned, entertainers rank as stewards. You will take your orders from the Chief Steward and do such entertaining and in such places as he directs. Now get out.'

'Yes, sir,' said George, feeling this a welcome turn in the conversation.

He stumbled from the cabin, falling over the Staff Captain.

'By God, Harry,' Captain Kettlehorn greeted his shipmate. 'I don't know what we're coming to. I've spent forty years at sea, starting as a bun-faced apprentice on food which would have disgraced a parsimonious workhouse and enjoying the care of a Chief Officer who could have given tips to Jack the Ripper. With hard work, single-mindedness, and application I passed my certificates and rose steadily through my profession. To what? To command something with about as much relation to a ship as one of the blasted boats in the Tunnel of Love at the Battersea Fun Fair.'

'Times are changing, Alfred,' murmured the Staff Captain, a little man with mild blue eyes. 'People have to be enticed—'

'Passengers should board a ship because they

want to go somewhere,' declared Captain Kettlehorn. 'Not to ardle-fardle round the ocean stuffing themselves with grub and booze, with a bit of how's-your-father on the offchance. Entertainers!' he snorted. 'When I first took command there was a ship's concert at the end of the voyage and you could generally dig up a couple of ladies to play the piano and sing on Saturdays. Nobody asked for any more. Now they fill the damn ship with ill-mannered riff-raff from the Charing Cross Road, whom I wouldn't have signed on as f'c's'le hands in the old days. Full to the eyes with drugs, too, I shouldn't be surprised.'

'Head Office—' muttered the Staff Captain.

'Head Office is mad,' Captain Kettlehorn dismissed it. 'As for that pip-squeak young Fitzhammond, he'd be very much better employed in a ladies' hairdressing establishment.' He threw himself into a chair. 'Any queries?'

'We've got an extra passenger, that's all, Alfred. Mr. Fitzhammond's young sister. Head Office want you to keep an eye on her. I gather she's in a bit of a state. She's just had some sort of difficult emotional experience.'

CHAPTER THIRTEEN

'Uncle,' asked Teddy Brickwood, 'what did you do in the War?'

'The what? The which? The War?' Lord Brickwood gave a jump. 'But my dear boy!' He raised a quick smile and screwed back his monocle. 'You mustn't worry your head about that sort of thing. The War's ancient history now. Why, we've not only long ago forgiven all our enemies, but we're even starting to pardon our friends.' The ormolu clock on the drawing-room mantelpiece struck four. 'What on earth's happened to Alastair and the tea?' he asked. 'Be a good lad, and go and chase them up a bit in the kitchen.'

'But you said the staff could go off,' Teddy reminded him. 'Even Dawn's disappeared.'

'So I did, so I did. I thought it would make our little party tonight more intimate. Only a few people are coming, of course—Sir George Peach, the General, and one or two others from the Club. I fancy we can refresh ourselves adequately from an informal buffet of whisky and *pâté de foie gras*. Stakes may become a little high, and I've discovered gentlemen prefer to lose money out of sight of the domestics. Surely you know how to play fan-tan?' he enquired, spreading a little pile of rice grains on the table in front of him.

'I've only read about it in novels, Uncle, when it always seems to be done by sinister-looking Chinamen.'

'Oh, dear me, no. Though there are enough sinister-looking Chinamen about, with all these Chinese restaurants springing up at every street corner. Chop suey and chips. Ugh!' He shuddered. 'Fan-tan, a game for which I have a great fondness, is one of much ingenuity and skill. I cover an unknown number of grains of rice with our upturned silver sugar-bowl,' he demonstrated. 'Removing the bowl, I now scrape away the grains in lots of four with the edge of this ivory letter-opener, thus...' Teddy watched expectantly as the pile was reduced. 'Leaving behind, as you will quickly appreciate, either three, two, one, or no grains of rice. One bets on this number beforehand.'

'Yes?' asked Teddy.

'That's the game,' said his uncle, rather impatiently. 'It is extremely popular in the night life of Macao. I plan shortly to make it the rage of London.'

A silence fell. Lord Brickwood sat fiddling about with his rice and his letter-opener. In his armchair, Teddy returned his eyes to the manuscript of an American novel eight hundred pages long about the sex life of people in some sort of religious community in Arizona. He'd got to an interesting but rather complicated bit about one of the ladies and her psychiatrist, but his eyes fell sightless on the typewritten page. Things were weighing on his mind. Teddy was a trustful young man, but there had arisen a little cloud out of the sea, like a policeman's hand.

In the week since he had announced his engagement to Grace Prothero, Uncle Horatio seemed to have suffered a personality change. He was his jovial and generous self in flashes, to be sure, but he had taken to moodiness, irritability, and escaping from the crowded flat dictating to Dawn in his bedroom. Teddy felt all this might be written off as acclimatization or indigestion, but he hardly expected such conduct from a man whose feet had recently been directed into a lifetime of bliss. He remembered when he'd first hitched up with Abigail he'd gone barging about the place sighing like furnace and writing ballads to her eyebrow, but he supposed with advancing years you took these things rather more calmly. Possibly the old boy was pining for Mrs. Prothero, he wondered, now she was back in Edinburgh to rev up preparations for the wedding. Uncle Horatio certainly put in some pretty expensive phone calls up north, though it was odd, Teddy, felt, recalling his own outpourings, he'd never thought of writing to her.

The next stop on Teddy's train of thought was Abigail. After that lunch with McInch he'd been firmly intending to put his uncle squarely in the Abigail picture but somehow the occasion never arose. You know how it is. You may have some whacking confession to make to your nearest and dearest, but when life is flowing along jollily it seems a pity to spoil it, and when it isn't you don't feel much inclined to make things worse. And anyway he wanted to raise first the question of those considerable funds being transferred from Hong Kong. But a couple of days ago he'd spotted a paragraph in the morning paper on the page labelled PEEP'S DIARY, one of those gossip columns supposed to be penned by some terribly smart and sophisticated knowing chap, which are really slung together on a junior sub-editor's desk over bottled beer and crisps at midnight. It said simply:

'Abigail Fitzhammond, Ban the Bomb daughter of the shipping and hotel magnate, believes in taking busmen's holidays. I hear she is now aboard her father' luxury liner *Snowdonia* cruising off the coast of Africa. The *Snowdonia* privides its passengers with all amenities, even a satirical night-club. George Churchyard, the Oxford undergraduate who crossed swords with television philosopher Professor Needler, has been engaged at a huge fee to keep Abigail and everyone else on board amused.'

'So that's it!' Teddy had muttered. 'As I jolly well thought.'

He was normally an easy-going young man, who rather than going through fire and water for his objectives in life preferred to take the signposted diversion for light traffic. Screwing up the beastly newspaper and kicking it into the corner, he had cursed himself bitterly for not storming Abigail's home, and crunching butlers underfoot dragging her kicking and screaming into a lifetime of happiness. He had blackly resolved to disembowel his old friend George on return to port, or at least have a pretty sharp word with him. Teddy now gave a sigh in memory of the galling piece of news, and tried to put it out of his mind by turning back to the things that religious lady was getting up to with her psychiatrist.

Then there were the cables, he remembered sharply before he'd managed to read another couple of lines. His uncle was out when the first one arrived from his father, saying simply, AMAZED HORATIOS APPEARANCE LONDON YESTERDAY DONT SIGN STOP FLYING IMMEDIATELY NASSAU BAHAMAS GUEST SCRUTCHINGS OF SCRUTCHINGS BOOKS INC AFFECTIONATELY FATHER. Teddy had thought deeply and replied c/o SCRUTCHINGS NASSAU DONT SIGN WHAT, to which had come the answer DONT SIGN ANYTHING. Finding the correspondence a bit mystifying, not to mention expensive, he'd let things slide until the afternoon Uncle Horatio and Mrs. Prothero plighted their troth.

Slipping round to the post office in Knightsbridge afterwards, he shot off, DELIGHTED TELL YOU UNCLE HORATIO TODAY BECAME ENGAGED TO BE MARRIED STOP BRIDE CHARMING WIDOW OBVIOUSLY MUCH LOVE WEDDING IMMINENT STOP DO YOU WISH COME HOME STOP ANY MESSAGE HAPPY PAIR TEDDY. He'd collected the reply at the door the next morning. GOOD GOD STOP GO STAY AUNTIE MAUD CHELTENHAM STOP REMAINING HERE SEVERAL MONTHS FATHER.

Difficult, Teddy thought, to spot what was behind it exactly. But something he felt was definitely lurking.

Finally, there was that other cutting now in his wallet. An earnest reader of PEEP'S DIARY, Teddy had spotted that morning, 'I can reveal to you the engagement of Lord Brickwood. He is to marry soon Mrs. Grace Prothero, widow of the nut and bolt tycoon. I was surprised to hear Lord Brickwood had slipped back to this country. At the end of the War he was the centre of the famous Brickwood Case, which caused the resignation of several junior ministers in the new Government. Lord Brickwood was a famous *bon viveur* of the 'thirties, a backer of many West End shows and the close friend of Elaine Norrimer and other famous actresses. After he was cashiered he left permanently for the Far East.'

'Uncle,' Teddy suddenly burst out, tossing

106

the manuscript aside. 'There was something in the morning paper—'

'Oh, you cut it out, did you? I thought it might be Alastair. He's always snooping round for something with a possible cash value.'

'But Undle Horatio!' cried Teddy. 'What does it all mean? I've heard the Brickwood Case mentioned once or twice in the family, of course, but Father always explained it was something to do with speeding.'

'My boy—' Uncle Horatio rose slowly from the table. He reached for a cigar. 'My boy, you have achieved man's estate,' he declared solemnly. 'Indeed, you are on the verge of matrimony and founding a family of your own.' He clipped the end as he started pacing slowly up and down the drawing-room. 'The time has come when you must know the plain truth about your uncle.' He struck a match. 'I am one of the great martyrs of history.'

'Oh, yes?'

'Captain Dreyfus, Admiral Byng, Cardinal Wolsey,' observed Lord Brickwood, puffing out smoke, 'All of us victims of jealousy and intrigue in the highest places.'

'I say,' exclaimed Teddy. 'I'm terribly sorry.'

Lord Brickwood raised a hand. 'I only ask you to hear my story. After that, my boy, I would only want you to judge me as you wish. As you know, I was never one of those layabout aristocrats,' he intoned. 'Not once did I desire to pass my days shooting and fishing on some totally inaccessible and probably highly uncomfortable country seat, living off my inheritance. Absolute parasites, those sort of people. No wonder the House of Lords has such a bad name. No, Teddy, I was public spirited. I had imagination. I wished to put my capital to use, providing jobs for our workpeople, the benefits of technology and the arts for our populace, and lasting benefit for our country.'

Teddy nodded enthusiastically.

'So I steeped myself in sordid commerce. I will not bore you, my boy, with details of my ventures in the days before you were born. They were many and often highly interesting. Then came the War. Although I was at the time involved in highly complicated financial transactions, I did my duty. I slipped away from London secretly and joined His Majesty's Royal Artillery, offering myself to be posted overseas at the earliest possible moment.'

Uncle Horatio flicked off his ash.

'I was a good soldier, I hope,' he observed modestly. 'I never flinched from my orders. I rose rapidly through the ranks, then I was honoured with His Majesty's Commission.' He straightened his shoulders. 'I trust I served my regiment loyally and bravely. No, Teddy, you need have no shame at your uncle's conduct throughout that long and bloody struggle, now so thankfully passing into the pages of history.'

'Were you out in Africa?' asked Teddy eagerly. 'El Alamein, and all that?'

'Actually, I spent most of the War at Willesden,' revealed Lord Brickwood, inspecting the end of his cigar. 'As you are aware, modern warfare is a complicated business calling impartially for many skills. The officer in charge of the stores—for such was I— is equally important as the battery commander in the field.'

'Oh, of course,' Teddy admitted politely.

'Willesden was a happy posting,' Lord Brickwood reminisced. 'For it allowed me to re-establish my commercial contacts in London. Business was very weird in those days, Teddy. With such a shortage of solid commodities one dealt only in such insubstantial items as clothing coupons and pig permits. But they were valuable times for me. Like many men in the Forces, my outlook matured. I hit upon a fundamental economic truth. It is, my boy, that governments at the beginning of a war are eager to buy scrap metal to turn into guns and tanks, which at the end of it they are equally eager to dispose of as scrap metal again. Thus I was doing a service to my country when I was able to use contacts in influential places· to sell off various howitzers and other equipment after our Forces had won victory. The terms of the sale were most advantageous to the Government, I will emphasize. All I had myself was a modest commission to cover my pains and one or two gifts I felt inclined to bestow. I regarded it then—I still regard it now—as a patriotic act.'

'Then what on earth was the fuss about?' asked Teddy, puzzled.

'Oh, there was some technicality. I was not demobilized at the time, and the guns were said to be still in use by some regiment or other. It was pure jealousy that caused my court martial. Half the Army was on the fiddle in one way or another at the time. When I came out of the Scrubs—there was some nominal sentence imposed, about eighteen months I think, allowing for remission—I set out undaunted to make another fortune in the Bountiful Orient.'

The doorbell rang.

'Do go and answer it, dear boy,' said Lord Brickwood wearily. 'After all that soul-baring I really feel I shall have to lie down.'

His mind buzzing like an overturned beehive, Teddy opened the front door to discover a severe-looking man in a bowler.

'Lord Brickwood?' he asked.

'He's—he's indisposed,' replied Teddy.

'Indeed? I am from Thrushington's of St. James's, the wine and spirit dealers. I should be much obliged if his Lordship would attend to this account without delay.'

'Account?' Teddy frowned. 'But surely you just bung them in at the end of the month?'

'Exactly. But in his Lordship's case we felt

disinclined to extend credit. We made it clear our vanman was to accept cash, but it appears his Lordship diverted him with some story of his nephew taking responsibility for payment.'

'Eh?' Teddy jumped. He became aware of a fat fellow with a big moustache in the background. 'And what do you want?' he asked shortly.

'The same as my friend here,' the fat man nodded. 'I'm from Sally Sims, the flower people. Our managing director knew Lord Brickwood when she was in the A.T.S.'

'I do wish you'd both clear off.' What with the strain of his uncle's confessions, Teddy was starting to lose his temper. 'We are not in the habit in my family of having duns crowding round our doors.'

'Oh? Really?' demanded the severe bird. 'Well, I'm afraid like a lot of other people in the affluent society you'll have to start getting used to it.'

'If you don't push off I'll jolly well send for the porter and get him to evict you.'

'Now look here, young feller me lad—' started Sally Sim's henchman.

'Get out!' commanded Teddy, trying to shut the door.

Something of an argument started, interrupted by the appearance of Lord Brickwood from the bedroom.

'Gentlemen, gentlemen!' he exclaimed. 'What

on earth is going on? Are you canvassing for a political party or something? I assure you I am a lifelong Liberal. Oh, these trifling bills,' he remarked, when things were explained to him. 'I must apologize for overlooking them, but I am somewhat preoccupied at the moment with plans for my forthcoming marriage to Mrs. Prothero, the widow of Prothero's Ironfoundries, you know. Teddy, do show them the cutting—only the top half is of interest. I will of course settle the accounts just as soon as Miss Turnpenny, my secretary, comes in tomorrow morning. I'm sorry you had the inconvenience of calling.'

This seemed to calm down the two purveyors, who shortly afterwards sloped off, though not without a growl or two in which the word 'Summons' could be made out.

Teddy shut the door and started at once, 'Uncle, after something one of those men said about me and his bill, I think I ought—'

'Please, Teddy,' Lord Brickwood cut in, relighting his cigar and absently dropping the bills into the waste-paper basket. 'A gentleman does not harp on unpleasant scenes. Just put those two counter-jumpers out of your mind. We have many more agreeable things to think about.'

'But Uncle!' Teddy banged the table. 'I must get it absolutely straight with you—'

'Dear boy, now you're being tedious.'

'I should have told you days ago, Uncle, that I am not in fact going to get—'

'See who it is this time,' interrupted Lord Brickwood crossly, as the doorbell rang again. 'If it's another bill say I've gone back to Hong Kong.'

Teddy discovered outside a large woman in a hat with bits of fruit on it, and a little man in a fawn raincoat.

'Yes?' he snapped.

'Where is he?' started the woman.

'Who the devil might you be?'

'Mr. and Mrs. Turnpenny,' replied the woman. 'From Petts Wood.'

'That's it,' said the man.

'I want to see that Lord Brickwood. Personal.'

'I'm afraid you can't possibly—'

'It's about our daughter, Dawn.'

'That's it,' said the man.

'To whom he has been making indecent suggestions,' added the woman, her fruit beginning to waggle rather.

'I really can't understand what you're talking about.'

'And moreover he hasn't paid her any wages.'

'That's it,' said the man.

Another argument developed. Voices were raised. People started opening the door of other flats.

'Now, now, now, now,' said Lord

113

Brickwood, reappearing as Teddy struggled to shut the door again. 'What a terrible fuss. Who have I the honour of addressing, madam? What a perfectly charming hat.'

'Mrs. Turnpenny, that's who you're addressing.'

'That's it,' said the man.

'Turnpenny ... Turnpenny ...' Lord Brickwood was lost in thought.

'Dawn's mum.'

'Dawn? Oh, Dawn. My most excellent and efficient secretary. The girl is not here, I'm afraid. I gave her the afternoon off.'

'She's at home safe and sound and thank the Lord for that,' snapped Mrs. Turnpenny, wagging her fruit at him. 'She's been telling me things.'

'That's it,' said the man.

'Things?' asked Lord Brickwood blankly.

'Indecent suggestions,' rolled out Mum, with relish.

Lord Brickwood appeared shocked.

'And no wages, neither.'

'That's it,' said the man.

'Teddy,' remarked Lord Brickwood chidingly, turning his gaze on his nephew. 'You've been a naughty boy.'

'What?' Teddy gave another jump.

Lord Brickwood laughed. 'I am afraid, Mrs. Turnpenny, that in your daughter's emotional state she did not put the facts entirely

accurately. I have noticed that your daughter—
such an attractive and charming young girl, and
so like yourself—held an absolute fascination for
my young nephew here. I have, Teddy,' he
added coyly, 'overheard one or two things. Eh?
I assure you, Mrs. Turnpenny, that he is a
young man of sterling character. I can vouch
personally for his most honourable intentions.
Anything in the slightest indecent was simply
misconstrued in the flirtatious atmosphere. I am
myself, as you see, a man of some years. And
moreover I am about to be married, to Mrs.
Prothero, widow of the Chairman of Prothero's
Ironfoundries—'

'I'm not satisfied,' the woman objected.

'That's it,' said the man.

'I think, Teddy, you and I had better have a
little chat,' Lord Brickwood continued, shaking
his finger. 'But youth, you know, Mrs.
Turnpenny. The hot fires—'

'Dawn says you asked her down to Brighton,'
complained Mum.

Uncle Horatio looked horrified. 'Brighton at
the Easter holidays? With all those crowds?
How preposterous!'

'Look here, Lord Brickwood—'

'My young nephew and I must have our heart
to heart,' declared Uncle Horatio, deftly pulling
Teddy inside and slamming the door. 'The fire
escape?' he hissed.

There was a good deal of banging on the door,

mixed with shouts of 'I am informing our solicitors' and 'That's it.'

'Through the kitchen,' Teddy gasped back.

'Let us slip away for a reviving whisky and soda in the calm air of my Club. It is better to leave by the back door anyway, I feel. I happen to have observed through the window the man from the Rolls Royce showroom engaged in some sort of discussion with our chauffeur.'

CHAPTER FOURTEEN

The Trafalgar Club in the middle of a warm May afternoon was calm to the point of sepulchral. Lord Brickwood threw himself into one the elephantine armchairs and announced, 'How utterly exhausting everyone seems to be today. Teddy, be a good lad and ring for the waiter.'

'Uncle,' announced Teddy, obliging but feeling pretty narked. 'I think I am entitled to an explanation.'

'Explanation, dear boy? What about?'

'About the story you told the woman in the funny hat.'

'Really, Teddy, you can't expect me to go into the nuance of all that before I've had a drink. I can assure you at once it was all done with the highest motives. Whisky and soda,' he ordered

116

from the arthritic waiter. 'Dear me, I must have left my wallet behind. Do you have a little change, Teddy? Perhaps you could let me borrow three or four of those fivers as well,' he added, as Teddy produced the remains of the fifty pounds his father had left for expenses. 'Thank you, dear boy. You will remind me about it, won't you?'

Lord Brickwood sat back, seeming disinclined for conversation. Teddy reached for *The Field* and scanned it all the way through forwards and backwards. He was wondering how to tell his relative he thought it a pretty poor show accusing him in public of fiddling about with a girl he wouldn't have touched with the end of a sterilized barge-pole, when Uncle Horatio abruptly drained his glass, rose to his feet, and announcing he had to write some important letters crossed to the writing desk in the corner and sat down.

The Trafalgar Club liked to furnish its members with everything they might need for their correspondence. There were six kinds of club paper of different sizes and colours, letter-cards, postcards, air-mail forms, telegraph pads, and black-edged sheets in case of need. In a trough waited half-a-dozen steel-nibbed pens, should you have forgotten your biro. Beyond the four shades of blotting-paper stood a spectrum of inks, and there were paper-clips, little green tags, sharp instruments for making holes, pen-wipers, rubbers, drawing-pins, tiny sponges, sealing-wax, pencil-sharpeners, an armoury of paper-knives, and some rather nice rulers.

None of these aids to composition seemed to stimulate Lord Brickwood. He just sat there, drawing little squiggles on the blotting-paper. He wrote a few words, then tossed them into one of the wastepaper baskets. He picked up elastic bands and made cat's-cradles. He reached for a paper-knife and started tapping his teeth. Teddy meanwhile read all the way through the *Sphere*, *Country Life*, and the *Illustrated London News*, and after trying to bury himself in *The Stateman's Yearbook* got up and stared idly out of the window.

The rush-hour tide was starting to ebb through Pall Mall, and he stood watching the passers-by with his mind prowling round the mysterious history of Uncle Horatio. Even in these days of broadminded morals, it comes as a psychological jar to any young man to discover that a near relative has done a stretch in the chokey. Still, Teddy reflected, his uncle had doubtless been the victim of that political skulduggery they used to satirize so keenly in *The Abattoir*. And after all, the nephews of John Hampden, the Count of Monte Cristo, and all Seven Bishops in the Tower must have found themselves in the same position. It was all years and years ago, he decided, and now that his uncle had done a smart phoenix the family could hardly afford not to overlook things and let those considerable funds *en route* from the East to Pott's Bank put everyone on their feet again.

Teddy suddenly became aware that one of the passers-by was passing-by a good many times. She was a slim middle-aged woman, who'd been rather at the make-up, wearing a floppy hat and some sort of furry animal which seemed to have crawled round her neck before succumbing to the mange. Every few turns she would stop and stare hard at the windows of the Club before resuming her sentry-go past the front steps. Odd, thought Teddy, edging behind the dusty velvet curtains. Possibly, he decided, she was idling away time while waiting for her husband or a bus. Or perhaps, it occurred to him, she was hoping to pick up one of the members. His speculation was cut short by Uncle Horatio throwing another sheet of writing-paper into the wastepaper basket and announcing, 'Teddy, be a good lad and order me another whisky. I'm sure I distinctly noticed the sun go over the yardarm.'

'Yes, of course, Uncle.' Teddy looked round for the arthritic waiter.

'Ring the bell, dear boy. It will produce some sort of service.'

The bell produced a brisk-looking man in a dark suit, with a bristly moustache and neat grey hair.

'Good afternoon,' Lord Brickwood greeted him genially, screwing in his monocle. 'How's the old complaint?'

'Lord Brickwood?' asked the brisk chap.

Uncle Horatio inclined his head. 'And who do I have the honour of addressing?'

'I am the Club Secretary.'

'My dear fellow, I am delighted to make your acquaintance. I am afraid, however, there are one or two things I feel it my duty to bring to your notice. The fish I ordered at luncheon last Monday was definitely off—'

'May I ask exactly when you were elected to the Club, Lord Brickwood?'

'Elected?' Lord Brickwood fiddled with his monocle cord. 'Really, it's becoming very difficult to say. In thirty-four, possibly? Thirty-five? Thirty-six? Things were so frightfully hectic and confused in those days, you know.'

'Lord Brickwood.' The brisk chappie clasped his hands behind him. 'Perhaps you could recall whom your proposer was?'

'You really can't expect me to remember at this distance,' he replied a little stuffily, taking out his cigar case. 'Perhaps you are aware that I have been abroad for several years? I rather fancy I was put up by Lord Keynes or Stanley Baldwin or someone like that.'

'It is my opinion, Lord Brickwood, that you have never been elected at all.'

'How dare you!' cried Uncle Horatio, his

120

monocle dropping in indignation. 'I have never been so—'

'There is nothing in the records, Lord Brickwood.'

'You know perfectly well the records were bombed during the war, you slanderous little twit.'

'Exactly, Lord Brickwood. That is why it has taken me some time to get the duplicates from the bank.'

'You can take it from me, Mr. Secretary, that I am going straight to my solicitors to take out a writ for—'

'As soon as your presence was reported in the Club, Lord Brickwood,' went on the Secretary evenly, 'the entire committee shook with horror, if not disbelief. I was instructed immediately to check your credentials, and then—'

'Your blasted committee's going to pay for this outrageous—'

'And then, to kick you out,' ended the secretary simply.

'You're mad. Stark staring mad.'

'Get out.'

'Mad!'

'At once, please, otherwise I shall summon assistance from the kitchen porters.'

Lord Brickwood rose. 'I refuse to stay in the place another second. I should have spotted before that it is merely a pothouse masquerading as a club for a large number of loafers masquerading as gentlemen. Come, Teddy! Where's my hat and stick?'

'But Uncle,' exclaimed Teddy in agitation, as they strode towards the front door. 'Surely you won't let him get away with language like that?'

'Get away with it? Of course he won't get away with it. Duff and Trimm will see to that, by jove! You wait till the scandal hits the papers. A few reputations will go up the spout, believe you me.'

'Of course, you're a member really? ' Teddy went on, in disbelief.

'Naturally, I am a member. Though I will admit to the possiblility of some genuine mistake having been made,' Uncle Horatio observed loftily as they reached the steps. 'I mean, I am possibly the member of some other club. They all look so terribly alike,' he pointed out with his stick. 'Tomorrow, perhaps,' he mentioned as an afterthought, 'we might look into that particularly hideous one across the way and find out. Gahhh!' he exclaimed, dropping his cane and his monocle at once.

'Horatio,' said the woman in the dead animal.

'Elaine,' croaked Uncle Horatio.

'What now?' asked Elaine, coming closer.

'Taxi!' said Lord Brickwood, grabbing his stick.

'Not so fast, Horatio. Surely you remember Ascot?'

'Ascot? Ascot? Teddy, get a cab. What Ascot? Which Ascot?'

'And all you said to me there?'

'My dear good woman, I have never set eyes on you in my life. I mean, dash it, Elaine,' he went on urgently, 'don't make a scene. Not here. Not right outside my Club, damn it.'

'You remember your last words, Horatio?' persisted Elaine, giving a smile.

'Last words? I don't remember any words. None whatsoever.'

'Oh dear, the memory of me has faded,' she sighed. 'But it is no matter. I have plenty of letters,' she explained, patting her handbag affectionately.

'My dear Elaine! I really must ask you to make any sort of complaint to my solicitors.'

'Your solicitors,' she mused. 'Duff and Trimm. Such overworked little men. But I'm not complaining, Horatio. I still want to marry you as desperately as ever.'

'*Pas—pas devant les enfants*,' muttered Uncle Horatio, jabbing his cane towards Teddy.

'But don't you want to marry *me* as desperately as ever, darling?'

'Really, I can't understand how you got this fantastic idea—'

'If you don't remember Ascot, Horatio,' Elaine remarked sweetly, 'perhaps you remember Torquay? Or Bognor Regis? Or Bath? Or Marlborough, Harrogate and

Worthing? Or Berwick-on-Tweed? The list's as long as the A.B.C.'

'This is all quite beside the point,' snapped Lord Brickwood. 'Thank God! A cab. I'll keep in touch,' he shouted, bundling Teddy in.

'I'll say you will,' Elaine called back from the pavement.

'Driver—drive on!' commanded Uncle Horatio, falling over Teddy in the back. He straightened himself up and stared nervously through the rear window. 'An old friend,' he explained, 'of the family.'

'Uncle,' declared Teddy, squaring his shoulders, 'It's time we got a few things straight.'

'Dear boy, for heaven's sake, can't you see I am in a state of considerable agitation and—'

'Who was that woman?' he demanded sternly.

'Elaine Norrimer,' said Uncle Horatio, trying to light his cigar. 'Used to be an actress. We were chummy off and on in the 'thirties. She seems to think I'm going to marry her. God knows why.'

'But you can't of course,' Teddy pointed out. 'Because you're going to marry Mrs. Prothero.'

'Exactly,' agreed Lord Brickwood, his hand shaking with the match. 'Not, I hasten to point out, Teddy, that Gracie is half the girl Elaine Norrimer was in her day. Or even now, I should think, for that matter. I wouldn't like you to imagine I had dubious taste in such matters. But of course, Mrs. Prothero's got the oof.'

'But surely, Uncle! Money can't enter into it, as far as you're concerned?'

'Well ... ah ... um...' observed Lord Brickwood, managing to produce a puff or two of smoke.

'I mean, all those considerable funds coming from the East?'

'I may have exaggerated slightly in front of that bank chappie,' admitted Lord Brickwood. 'I always believe it does no harm to generate confidence. As a matter of fact, the funds will not, just at this moment, be particularly large. The market has been rather unsettled in Hong Kong lately. Indeed, I should not be at all surprised if the funds did not appear at all.'

'But who's going to pay for all the food and drink and servants and things in the flat?' cried Teddy.

'That's simple,' replied Lord Brickwood, puffing more heartily. 'You.'

'Me?'

He nodded. 'Yes, once you're married to this Fitzhammond girl you'll be able to lay you hands on absolute millions.'

'But I'm not going to marry the Fitzhammond girl!'

'What!' Lord Brickwood bit through his cigar. 'You mean you jilted her?'

'Well, she jilted me, I suppose. Anway, she's gone off with a bloke called George.'

'Ye gods! You blasted idiot! What the hell do you think I came home for? Still owe for the fare as well,' he added.

'Where to, sir?' asked the driver through his partition.

'Queer Street,' said Lord Brickwood, and threw his cigar on the floor and stamped on it.

CHAPTER FIFTEEN

An hour or two after Teddy and Lord Brickwood drove away from the steps of the Trafalgar Club, Abigail Fitzhammond came on deck of the liner *Snowdonia* to lean against the rail, while the sun, tired out from another day of blazing away, hurried to sink itself in the cool waters of the Atlantic.

Astern lay the island of Tenerife, its inhabitants gleefully chalking up the takings from dolls dressed as duennas, silk scarves with bullfights on them, those castanet things which are so jolly difficult to play, bunches of rather tasty bananas, and cages of canaries which once aboard fell into a silent fit of the sulks. Ahead lay the island of Madeira, its inhabitants gleefully calculating the takings from wicker furniture quite impossible to sit on, little shiny barrels for sherry and biscuits in the parlour, baskets of oranges, and crates and crates of the

126

local booze. Tucked away in the passengers' cabins was a load of stuffed Barbary apes from Gibraltar, with leather pouffes and those Moorish slippers from Casablanca which keep dropping off. The *Snowdonia* had just reached the limits of her spring cruise and was turning towards home.

Abigail gave a deep sigh and threw a dreamy look towards the wake churning away beyond the stern. She gave another deep sigh and turned a second dreamy look along the line of lifeboats stretching towards the Verandah Café. At that moment she would have sighed deeply and looked dreamily at anything, even the Captain. For Abigail was hopelessly in love.

And not with Teddy Brickwood.

The girl was not unobserved. From the wing of the bridge the Captain was watching her closely through his glasses. He reflected that a voyage which he'd found as unbrokenly horrible as the Ancient Mariner's had at least left Miss Fitzhammond enjoying herself. And had it not been for his own discreet and fatherly manipulation behind the scenes that evening they left Gibraltar, the Captain congratulated himself, this apple of Mr. Fitzhammond's eye might now be eaten into by drug-taking maggots from the Charing Cross Road.

As Captain Kettlehorn strode back to the chartroom Abigail glanced round. Her face lit up. She had the feeling that someone had opened a warm bottle of soda-water inside her. Her beloved was approaching down the deck.

'Why, hello, there,' called Mervyn Spode.

'Hello,' breathed Abigail.

'Admiring the sunset?' asked Mervyn, moving in on the rail.

'It's beautiful,' said Abigail, dropping her eyes.

'Not a speck as beautiful,' observed Mervyn, twining their fingers together, 'as you.'

'Oh, Mervyn,' she melted.

'You are the sun in my heaven,' he pointed out. 'My moon, my stars, and all my planets,' he added.

'Oh, Mervyn!'

'My sunshine, my rain, my storms, my winds—zephyrs, that is.'

'Oh, *Mervyn*.'

Which proves she must have been pretty smitten, all this hardly being in the Shakespearian sonnet class.

Mervyn Spode had made Abigail's acquaintance early in the voyage.

'Steward!' he called as the *Snowdonia* was being fussed away from the Southampton dockside by grubby little tugs, like the old dears in cardigans you see backstage sticking pins in those dolled-up fashion models.

'Sir?' said Huffkins, on his way to collect the Captain's tobacco issue.

'My name's Mervyn Spode. I expect you've

128

heard of me.'

'Yes, sir,' agreed Huffkins politely.

'Any interesting passengers aboard?'

'Afraid I can't say, sir.'

'Among the ladies, you know,' went on Mervyn Spode, idly producing his wallet.

'I did hear, sir, up in the Captain's cabin, that Mr. Fitzhammond's daughter is with us this trip.'

'Is she, by jove!' Mervyn's delicately arched eyebrows quivered upwards. 'Thank you, steward,' he added, handing over ten bob.

'Very kind of you, sir.'

'And steward—'

'Sir?'

'If you could arrange for me to meet the young lady fairly soon, you will have the other half.'

'I'm sure that can be managed, sir.'

'Discreetly, of course.'

'Naturally, sir.'

'Thank you, steward.'

'Thank *you*, sir.'

Mervyn gave a little sigh. His employment at one time on one of the brighter newspapers had left him grasping the principle that cash handed out for private information is never wasted.

About an hour after the ship sailed Mervyn Spode was standing close against Abigail in the Verandah Café, with both his arms round her middle.

All British vessels being conducted on the assumption there is an iceberg lurking round every corner, the first event on board, though of course after the opening of the duty-free bar, is boat drill. Nobody on a British ship would contemplate slacking the turn-out, shipwrecks being one of the few remaining international events that we are rather good at. Even if you are the daughter of the owner of the line and determined to spend the voyage in your cabin reading all the way through *The Decline and Fall of the Roman Empire*, when the alarm bells sound you take your life-jacket and make your way frightfully calmly to your assembly point like everyone else.

The modern life-jacket has been cunningly reduced largely to holes and bits of tape, making it as tricky to don at the first shot as a space suit. Luckily, you encounter at this assembly point in the Verandah Café a deferential steward with a face like a dried walnut, who politely introduces you to a fair and delicate-looking young man in a stylish suit, who considerately helps you into the thing and ties neat little reef-knots on your midriff.

'I hope we shan't actually be swimming for it,' the young man observed, a wan smile flitting over his pale features. 'After all, I've only come on this cruise for my health.'

'Oh, really?' asked Abigail.

'The doctors insisted,' he added, seeming to

go paler. 'I'm afraid I'm rather frail.'

'Oh, dear,' said Abigail.

'Still, it'll be a chance to catch up on my work. I wonder if you've read my articles in the magazines, on interior decorating and so on? I'm Mervyn Spode,' announced Mervyn Spode.

'Yes, of course. I thought them frightfully clever.'

'How terribly sweet of you.' The wan smile flitted again. 'I should love to design a place for you. I thought at once you had such a reposed and sympathetic face. I believe one should always start with the *person*, you know. You would be the jewel. I should merely provide the setting.'

'Now you're just being flattering,' smiled Abigail. After all, you can't say much else when the chap has got both hands firmly in your armpits.

'Not at all,' returned Mervyn Spode, giving a few fiddles to the knots. 'Though I'm afraid I don't know you from Eve, as soon as I set eyes on you I told myself, "There at last is a face one could do something *with*".'

But Abigail was distracted by a scene through the wide scuttles of the Verandah Café. Out on deck was a man with gold braid and heavy eyebrows, whom she supposed was the Captain. Facing him was an unfortunate member of the crew in civvies, with his lifejacket tangled in one of those wire-rope things they used to swing out the lifeboats. There seemed to be some sort of argument, with the Captain shaking his fist and jumping up and down on the deck. Finally, a large sailor in a blue jersey appeared with a knife to cut the poor man free, and he was hustled away rapidly somewhere out of sight. The peculiar thing, Abigail thought, was the strung-up sailor looked exactly like Teddy Brickwood's nice friend George at Oxford.

'How strange,' she murmured to herself. 'Surely it couldn't be? I'm so sorry.' She turned to Mervyn. 'I didn't catch your last remark.'

'Please forgive me,' continued Mervyn soupily, 'but I simply can't prevent myself saying what remarkable eyes you have.'

The mild-eyed Staff Captain gave his little chat about everyone remembering the great British traditions of the sea and wrapping up warm in their woollies. Mervyn started untying all his reef-knots. Five minutes later he arranged to meet Abigail for a drink in the Shanty Bar after dinner.

Abigail strolled back to her suite on A deck pretty pensively. She was definitely a girl who liked to think that she thought. She hadn't wanted to go on a cruise, but her father insisted that her being *La Dame aux Camélias* over breakfast every morning was getting on his nerves. She would rather have waited in Berkeley Square for Teddy to call and make up that stupid argument about the fish. She'd cried like a squeezed orange on the train home from Oxford, but she utterly refused to start the reconciliatory ball rolling by sending tender little notes and things. Which just shows the difficulties when a pair of star-cross'd lovers find themselves up the creek, particularly such a pig-headed couple as this.

Abigail reflectively inspected the wardrobe unpacked by her personal stewardess. She'd intended to spend the evening catching up with her *Decline and Fall*, but this Mervyn Spode certainly seemed very helpful and charming. Though of course he hadn't anything like Teddy's intellectual capacity, she told herself firmly, picking her smartest Balmain.

Mervyn Spode was meanwhile pacing the boatdeck as The Needles disappeared astern, planning his tactics for the night.

'Why, Merv,' came a throaty voice behind him.

He pulled up short. He turned to find a girl with long blond hair and a patchwork dress with great blobs of coloured glass on it, smoking a cigarette in an affair like a pair of sugar-tongs slipped round her little finger.

'Er—I'm afraid I haven't had the pleasure—' said Mervyn quickly. His employment at one time in provincial repertory had left him with the art of masking his emotions.

'How's Caroline, Merv?' asked Morag.

'Caroline?' He gave a quick smile. 'I'm sorry,

133

but I've never had anyone of that name in my circle of acquaintances.'

'Now you're being utterly conspiratorial,' said Morag huskily. 'What on earth happened to your darling little antique shop in the King's Road? Now it sells those absolutely fabulous and quite uneatable pizza pie things.'

'Look, Morag—' Mervyn Spode licked his lips. 'I'd like you to know I've buried my past.'

'But darling! That would need an entire mausoleum.'

'I admit I've had my mistakes over the years—'

'Caroline was one of them,' observed Morag, puffing from her sugar-tongs.

'But I'm as entitled to a fresh start as much as the next man.'

'Oh, of course, darling. But why on earth do you want to make it on board this peculiar boat?'

'I'm travelling for the benefit of my health,' countered Mervyn firmly.

'But not for anyone else's, I bet.'

'Honestly, Morag—' Mervyn Spode directed on her the eyes which had melted female hearts like ices in a heat-wave. 'I've turned over a new leaf. You know how terribly delicate I've always been.' He gave a cough. 'Don't you remember, my awful turns?'

'Yes, darling. They completely ruined two of my parties.'

'The doctors tell me I may not have very much longer,' Mervyn revealed, looking as though body and soul were likely to fly apart any minute. 'I just want to spend the rest of my life utterly decently, that's all.'

'You're sure, darling,' murmured Morag, 'the shock itself won't kill you?'

'I know I've been a pretty bad type on and off in my time,' Mervyn Spode admitted frankly. 'But you will give me a chance, Morag, won't you? I mean, by not spreading round the ship all those stories about my past, which believe me I'm quite disgusted with.'

'Darling, what a rich vein of conversation I'll have to leave untapped.'

'Please, Morag . . . Just for the sake of the old days in the Cromwell Road.'

Morag gave a sigh. Under that hard and brittle exterior she was very much a two-and-a-half-minute egg. 'All right, darling. I'll keep mum.'

'That's terribly, terribly sweet of you. It's a real promise?'

'Cross my heart, darling.'

'I knew you'd never kick a man when he's down, Morag.'

'Not much point kicking him while he's still up, is there, darling?' Morag had another puff at her sugar-tongs. 'See you at bingo.'

CHAPTER SIXTEEN

The *Snowdonia* hastened away from her native shores, with everyone on board slipping into the usual routine of a British ship at sea. At eight in the morning stewards hurried round the cabins with pots of tea and slices of hot buttered toast. At nine a gong sounded for breakfast, with six sorts of cereal, three kinds of fish, eggs, bacon, sausages, chops, hamburgers, veal collops, curry, and marmalade. At eleven stewards hastened along the decks with steaming urns of bouillon and little salt crackers, and at twelve sharp everyone gathered in the Shanty Bar until the bugle blew for the six-course lunch. By four o'clock the stewards were hustling about with tea and cream cakes, at six the passengers gathered in the Shanty Bar again, at seven chimes rang out for the eight-course dinner, then everyone played bingo until the sandwiches appeared at ten. The weather was lovely, and all aboard seemed to be enjoying themselves.

Except Captain Kettlehorn.

'Chief Officer, blast your boots, where are you?' he shouted on the bridge the second morning out, as the ship sailed peacefully across the gently heaving bosom of a sleeping Bay of Biscay.

'Here, sir,' replied the Chief Officer,

appearing from the chartroom.

'Time for my social round,' grunted Captain Kettlehorn. 'Personally, I think a ship's captain should be heard and not seen. But if the Company insists I make an exhibition of myself from ten-thirty to eleven daily, who am I to object? What the devil do you want?' he demanded abruptly, as Morag appeared on the bridge wearing tight black trousers, a tighter black sweater, and a string of large white beads resembling human skulls.

'Darling, this is an absolutely divine spot for the treasure hunt,' she announced huskily.

'The—the what?'

'An awful bore, but the passengers are absolutely screaming for a treasure hunt. Do you think I could hide a thimble in that peculiar brass thing in front of the steering-wheel?'

'Will you get off my bridge instantly?' barked Captain Kettlehorn, his eyebrows seeming in danger of flying off by centrifugal force.

'But, darling—'

'Do not address the Master as "darling", dammit!'

'Now you're cross,' conceded Morag.

Captain Kettlehorn covered his face with his hands.

'Miss Aspinall,' he managed to say, 'I have been at sea for many, many years—'

'Yes, I'm sure, darling, there's more salt in your bones than an anchovy.'

'Miss Aspinall.' The Captain swallowed. 'I only ask you to assist the running of the vessel by recognizing that I have a job to do on board.'

'Oh, but so have I, darling. You can't imagine what a ghastly strain it is keeping all those dreadful people amused. They want nothing but anagrams, spelling-bees, beetle-drives, three-legged races, beauty competitions, improving lectures—'

'I realize, Miss Aspinall,' the Captain interrupted shakily, 'that you are carrying out with great conscientiousness your onerous duties as hostess. I only require you to do so without making use of my ruddy compass. Why not ask the Chief Engineer if you can do your blasted hunting in the engine room?'

'That's a thought,' agreed Morag, turning. 'Which of these ladder affairs is the way out?'

Captain Kettlehorn strode on to the wing of the bridge. He clasped his hands behind him. He stared aft along the passenger decks. He scowled. 'Ye gods,' he muttered. 'Forty years at sea! For what? To play ruddy hunt the slipper.'

His expression lightened slightly as he caught sight of young Miss Fitzhammond in a deckchair with a book. He was glad the girl had settled so easily into the ship. A bit of luck, he told himself, that young fellow Spode at his table was providing some companionship for her. Not a bad type at all, Spode. A bit airy-fairy, but well-mannered. He had listened respectfully to the Captain's story during lunch the previous day of the typhoon he'd weathered in the China Sea. At dinner, he'd listened equally attentively to the Captain's story of the iceberg he'd encountered in the Cabot Straits. And at one o'clock, the Captain anticipated with some pleasure, he would be able to enjoy the story of the boilers blowing up in the Persian Gulf.

Captain Kettlehorn quivered. There, approaching the young lady in the middle of the deck, was that horrible entertainer and drug-addict.

'Huffkins!' he roared in the direction of his private deck. 'Get that man up to my cabin this instant.'

George Churchyard was, in fact, the only person aboard apart from Captain Kettlehorn not enjoying the trip. During the two days at sea he'd found the members of the band with whom he shared his cabin snored a good deal and didn't much seem to wash their feet. He also discovered his duties as entertainer included such things as sorting the ship's mail, collecting the crew's dirty laundry, and polishing the ballroom deck. All this hadn't left him much time for a heart-to-heart with Abigail about Teddy Brickwood, which he'd decided upon as soon as Morag had breathed in his ear that Fabian's little sister was aboard.

'What the devil do you mean appearing on the

passenger decks in broad daylight?' the Captain now bristled at him in his cabin. 'Eh? Blast your boots.'

'I was just taking a little air,' George returned.

'Sir!'

'I was just taking a little air, sir,' he repeated a shade wearily.

'Attention!'

'If you must know,' George went on, feeling that after a couple of days' sailing the time had come to put the beastly fellow in his place, 'I was going on deck to have a word with Miss Fitzhammond.'

'What! Have you the barefaced insolence to admit you were about to molest—'

'I wasn't gong to molest,' George interrupted shortly. 'It so happens that Miss Fitzhammond is a personal friend of mine.'

'Ye gods!' The Captain drew breath. 'Listen to me, Churchyard—in my forty years at sea I have learned to be tolerant of many things. Insubordination, indiscipline, lying, stealing, and deceiving—all these I have suffered so much I am prepared to overlook their milder manifestations. But one thing I damn well will not stand, and that's an insult to my ruddy intelligence. Get me? If you want to think up some plausible lie, that's your worry. But to suggest to me that you, an out-of-work, down-at-heel, third-rate actor straight off the streets of

London, should be acquainted with the daughter of the owner of this Line, is nothing more than an outrageous affront to my capabilities as this vessel's commander. Though no doubt,' the Captain was prepared to concede, 'your mental processes are considerably deranged through your habit of taking drugs. Huffkins.'

'Sir?'

'Escort this man to his quarters. I don't want to see you talking to a passenger for the rest of the voyage, Churchyard. Understand, blast your boots?'

'I've got to talk to them all tonight,' countered George surlily. 'It's my first performance.'

'That is a matter of your official duties. Now get out.'

Abigail, curled in her deckchair, was already aware of the presence on board of George Churchyard, the best friend of an Oxford undergraduate with whom she had once had a pallid and youthful affair. An Oxford undergraduate who paled to a shadow in the lovelight compared with Mervyn Spode, the man who had been writing her poetry, saying how she'd saved his delicate life, and on and off chewing her hair eighteen hours a day solidly since leaving port. It's well known there's nothing like the sea and the stars and the phosphorescence on the waters to make love grow like forced rhubarb. It's always happening aboard ships. Besides, I suppose the passengers have got to find something to do between all those meals. And that's not to mention Abigail being on the rebound like a well-hit squash ball.

Abigail's heart now fluttered like a netted butterfly at every soft-footed approach of Mervyn Spode. All she could remember of Teddy was his never so much as tasting a mouthful of her hair in her life. And the ruddy ship hadn't even reached Gibraltar.

That same evening Abigail held Mervyn's hand sitting at the back of the First Class ballroom, while George mounted the stage to give his first performance afloat. He was feeling a little happier with his lot. He had his piano and his lights. He had on his dinner-jacket. He had an audience. And any actor deprived for long of an audience feels like a chap trying to play tennis by himself.

'Good evening, ladies and gentlemen,' George began, playing a few bars. He was pleased to see a pretty good turn-out in the ballroom, there not being any bingo, with members of the crew off duty crowding round the back. 'I should like to tell you a little story,' George went on, 'about a Red Indian Chief. He was very rich and civilized Indian Chief, and he had three squaws—'

'Bless my boots, the blasted feller's started,' came a growl from the front of the stalls.

'I told the deck quartermaster not to cast off

until you arrived, Alfred,' added the mild-eyed Staff Captain, following Captain Kettlehorn across everybody's legs to their seats in the middle of the front row.

'The Indian Chief himself slept in a big double bed,' George continued from the piano. 'But the three squaws followed the old tribal custom of—'

'I'm so sorry madam,' apologized Captain Kettlehorn hoarsely, stumbling over somebody's nylons.

'That's quite all right, Captain.'

'Harry, tell the Quartermaster to have these seats further back next time.'

'Certainly, Alfred.'

'—sleeping on hides on the floor. The first squaw slept on a lion's hide. The second squaw slept on a zebra's hide—'

There was a piercing note as Captain Kettlehorn, comfortably settled in his seat, blew through his pipe.

'And the third squaw slept on a hippopotamus' hide. In the fullness of time the squaw who slept on the lion's hide produced a son—'

'I know this story, Harry,' George and everyone else overheard.

'Oh, do you, Alfred? Is it funny?'

'Not in the slightest,' said Captain Kettlehorn.

'—Shortly after, the squaw who slept on the

143

zebra's hide also produced a son. And a little later the squaw who slept on the hippopotamus' hide produced twin sons—'

'Drugs, y'know,' observed Captain Kettlehorn.

'Drugs, Alfred?'

'Him up there,' Captain Kettlehorn indicated with his eyebrows.

'Which proves the squaw on the hippopotamus is equal to the sum of the squaws on the other two hides,' ended George.

He played a little trill on the piano. This was the only sound.

'I don't think I see the point, Alfred,' complained the Staff Captain.

'There isn't one,' said Captain Kettlehorn.

'Do you know the definition of an alcoholic?' persisted George, with a fixed smile. 'Somebody you dislike intensely who drinks the same amount as you do.'

One or two of the passengers laughed at that one. Captain Kettlehorn struck a match and lit his pipe.

'Or the definition of a sadist?' George persevered, slightly encouraged in spite of the smoke-screen going up between him and the audience. 'A sadist is somebody who's terribly nice to a masochist.'

'Wish the feller would speak up,' the Captain snorted. 'Can't hear a word.'

'Then there was the man who went into a pub

for a drink,' George lumbered on between tinkles on the piano, deciding to try something more simple. 'While he wasn't looking the landlord's dog took his hat into the corner and ate it. "Look what your dog's done to my hat," the man complained. "Well, that's your fault for leaving it here," replied the landlord. So the man said, "I don't like your attitude." And the landlord replied, "Oh, no. It's *your* 'at 'e chewed," ha, ha,' ended George.

'Ye gods,' muttered the Captain.

'And now,' announced George, jumping from the piano stool, 'I should like to give you my impression of the Prime Minister.'

The Prime Minister was his shot in the locker. It had gone over a treat in *The Abattoir*, and even in the Harem Club had raised a guffaw from the bar. But somehow the passengers on a cruise didn't throw themselves all over the decks in hysterics. Possibly, wondered George, as he went on doggedly in silence, they felt detached afloat from such grim realities as prime ministers. Or perhaps, it struck him, it was simply the Captain rising from his seat in the first minute and after announcing loudly, 'I've had about enough of this rubbish,' stamping his way across everybody's feet again towards the exit.

'Ladies and gentlemen, I should now like to give my next imitation,' declared George, feeling pretty fed up as he ended to a desultory clap and even a whistle or two from the back. 'Somebody you know very well,' he continued, deciding to plump for the Archbishop of Canterbury rather than Mao Tse-tung. 'Somebody who—'

There was a burst of applause as Morag appeared on the stage, particularly as she was wearing a shiny gold dress which looked as if it had been put on with a paint-spray.

'*Eyebrows*, darling,' she murmured, handing him something on a bit of elastic. 'From the Devil set in the fancy-dress box. Utterly satanic.'

'Morag, really—' muttered George in confusion.

'The *Captain*, darling,' she smiled.

'But Morag, I'm in the middle of a show—'

'Imitate *him*, darling,' she advised briefly, tripping off again. 'You'll absolutely *send* them.'

'Good lord, of course!' exclaimed George. 'Ladies and gentlemen,' he announced at once. 'Somebody who you know very well. Blast my boots, stand to attention when you address the Master...'

Marching towards the bridge Captain Kettlehorn paused as a roar of laughter split the calm night like his boilers blowing up in the Persian Gulf. Waves of joyful sound rolled towards him for minutes on end from the direction of the First Class ballroom. He rested his hand on the bridge ladder and raised his

146

eyebrows. He seemed to have missed the best part of the show.

CHAPTER SEVENTEEN

'That was a terrific bit of quick thinking on your part last night, Morag,' said George gratefully.

'But darling, it was an absolute *natural*. I'm sure those beasts are utterly savage and absolutely teeming with vermin,' she went on.

It was the following afternoon, and they stood in the blazing sunshine half-way up the Rock of Gibraltar, inspecting the apes which keep British rule in the place.

'That one looks just like a certain professor I knew at Oxford,' remarked George.

He indicated one of the more bristly ones, busy chewing the windscreen wipers off a parked car, while a dozen of the *Snowdonia*'s passengers jostled round trying to photograph it.

'Poor apes!' sighed Morag. 'Don't you think animals feel ever so much safer when they've got the humans behind a row of great thick bars?'

Tiring of the apes, they turned to lean over the roadside parapet. They gazed for some time at the sparkling bay with the ship anchored far below and the airstrip jutting out to sea like a giants' diving-board.

'Darling,' asked Morag huskily, breaking the silence. 'Do you like making promises?'

George laughed. 'I don't think I've made any since I got drummed out of the Boy Scouts.'

'I hate making them.' She adjusted the gold-mounted snake round her neck. 'It always upsets me so terribly when I have to break them.'

Morag slipped back into a moody silence. It seemed to George the girl had something on her mind. Or was it, he wondered a little more warmly, that she was starting to notice his finer qualities? For Morag, he reflected, though she tended to go about looking like a left-over from the Chelsea Arts Ball, was undoubtedly a dish.

George's reflections were broken by the noise of a car horn as a large limousine pushed through the sightseers on the narrow road. In the back were Abigail and Mervyn.

'Odd how Abigail Fitzhammond's taken up with the bloke who's so skinny he won't go in the swimming-pool,' he remarked.

'You know that dear little girl with all the money pretty well, don't you, darling?' asked Morag throatily.

George nodded. 'She was engaged to a chum of mine at Oxford. They got off the launching-pad with a fine flourish, but somehow they didn't manage to get into matrimonial orbit.'

Morag idly traced patterns on the parapet with her three-inch finger-nails, which had now gone green.

'This chum—was he a nice man, darling?'

'One of the best,' replied George firmly. 'They had some stupid row one afternoon and broke it up. A pity, because they suited each other just like stilton and celery. I'd gone down to Fabian's office that day to negotiate an armistice, but I'm afraid I didn't get very far. Though once this cruise affair is over and they see each other again,' he ended confidently, 'I guarantee they'll fall into each other's arms like a couple of goal-scoring soccer forwards.'

There was another silence while Morag inspected the view.

'Darling,' she announced, 'just for you I'm going to do something dreadful.'

'Dreadful?' asked George, for the moment alarmed she was going to chuck herself off the Rock.

She nodded. 'Yes, I'm going to break a really proper cross-your-heart promise. But some utterly ghastly sort of tragedy's about to happen.'

'Tragedy?'

'Something that would make King Lear look like Jimmy Edwards.'

'Not the Captain?' he asked, more hopefully. 'A stroke, perhaps?'

Morag shook her head, rattling the snake.

'That man Mervyn Spode.'

'Oh, your friend—'

149

'No friend of mine, darling. Though in his time he'd made more passes at me than in the entire Alps. He's a perfectly bestial man. A vampire. Quite exsanguinating,' She shuddered. 'Now he's got dear little Abigail firmly by the jugulars.'

'But surely, Morag!' George laughed. 'You're not suggesting a nice and extremely sensible young woman like Abigail would really get mixed up with a fellow she's only met on board?'

'Mixed up, darling? They're utterly entwined.'

George stared. 'I just can't believe it.'

'Worse things happen at sea, darling,' observed Morag throatily.

'Then I'd better do something about it,' George frowned. 'Pretty sharpish, too.'

'I'll say, darling. Before the fangs get utterly embedded.'

'Poor Teddy!' muttered George.

'You might mention to her,' suggested Morag, 'that next time Merv has her against the rails chewing bits of her hair, she should enquire about the health of dear Caroline.'

The *Snowdonia* was leaving Gibraltar that evening when George, tearing himself away from his laundry collecting, made his way determinedly up the main companionway to seek out Abigail. He owed it to Teddy, he told himself as he hurried aloft, to tell the girl firmly

150

that this fellow Spode, who had been doing so much breathing down her neck, was nothing but an unprincipled sponger whom Bluebeard would have shunned in the club. Further, he would point out, the sun of the affections in which Abigail now basked shone on girls like it does on Margate beach during August Bank Holiday. And that wasn't to mention Caroline in particular.

On the bridge, Captain Kettlehorn was in charge of operations leaving port. An uneasy mood lay upon his epauletted shoulders. The passengers and crew had been behaving in a peculiar manner since their arrival at Gibraltar.

The usual reaction of the ship's company to his approach was hiding behind some convenient structure, watching nervously if the storm would pass by or pause to rain down thunderbolts. Now they simply stood and grinned. Strange, thought Captain Kettlehorn. At first he suspected he had some portion of his dress improperly adjusted, but Huffkins assured him he was well turned out fore and aft. He now began to wonder if mutiny was afoot, and whether to send a signal to the Royal Navy before it was too late and he'd be sailing into the Atlantic to get his throat cut.

'Two points to starboard,' he commanded the helmsman. 'Blast your boots, man! Wake up! Do you want to put the ruddy ship slap on the end of the Rock?'

He turned as he heard a snigger behind him. It was the mild-eyed Staff Captain.

'Really, Staff! I fail to see how the vessel running ashore can be the subject of the slightest levity.'

The Staff Captain gave another giggle. Captain Kettlehorn's eyes flashed round the bridge. His eyebrows shot up. All his officers were staring at him with stupid smirks on their faces.

'I am totally unable to understand,' he barked, 'why everyone on board has suddenly started staring at me like a bunch of half-drunken village idiots. It is not only extreme bad manners, but lacking the respect required by the Master of a seagoing vessel.'

The Staff Captain started laughing so much he had to grab the binnacle for support.

'Damnation!' roared Captain Kettlehorn. 'Won't somebody explain this tomfoolery?'

'It—it was the imitation,' the Staff Captain managed to get out. 'So absolutely lifelike, you know.'

'Imitation? Imitation? What blasted imitation?'

'By that clever young fellow Churchyard. After you'd left last night. Had us absolutely in fits. Terribly good, wasn't it, Chief?'

'Yes, sir,' grinned the Chief Officer at Captain Kettlehorn. 'He's a real asset to the ship, sir. He'll keep the passengers amused all right till we're back at Southampton.'

'He really was jolly funny, sir,' piped up the Third Officer. 'It's a pity you weren't there to see it, sir.'

'If I may say so,' added Huffkins, who had appeared with coffee and sandwiches, 'the stewards' mess thought it a real treat, sir.'

'Quartermaster!' bellowed Captain Kettlehorn.

'Sir?'

'Two deckhands and follow me. Staff! You're in charge up here.'

With three sailors at his heels Captain Kettlehorn clattered down the main companionway. He met George hurrying up.

'You there! Churchyard!' The Captain quivered to a stop. 'I'm putting you on a criminal charge.'

'Charge? What charge?' asked George confusedly, his mind filled with his coming conversation with Abigail.

'Incitement to mutiny,' returned Captain Kettlehorn crisply. 'Quartermaster! Take that man below.'

'Look here,' protested George crossly. 'I happen to have a highly important message to deliver to Miss Fitzhammond—'

'Quartermaster, search him carefully for drugs. Compliments to Chief Steward, he's to be worked in the galley washing up for the remainder of the voyage.'

'Hey!' exclaimed George, as the deckhands seized him by the arm. 'You can't do that.'

'I can do anything I like, blast your bleeding boots. You ought to have read the ship's articles before you signed 'em in the Super's office. Inform Chief Steward, Quartermaster, no tobacco issue and to stop his tap. And if I see your nauseating features outside the crew's quarters once again before we reach Southampton,' the Captain ended to George, 'I shall have very great pleasure bashing them in with a marlin spike. Quartermaster, take his feet.'

'What on earth's going on?' asked Abigail, coming down the companionway with Mervyn.

'Some sailor giving trouble, I should imagine,' he told her. 'They all get terribly drunk ashore, you know.'

'Whoever he is, I hope they won't hurt him,' Abigail added, glimpsing George's arms and legs disappearing down aft.

'You know, you're so deliciously tender-hearted,' murmured Mervyn, taking her hand. 'Even towards riff-raff.'

'Oh, Mervyn,' responded Abigail, dropping her eyes.

'Come,' he suggested. 'Let us be alone together in some quiet corner of the deck. I've just composed a little poem that I'd rather like you to hear.'

'Oh, Mervyn,' said Abigail.

CHAPTER EIGHTEEN

'Let us not be downhearted,' declared Uncle Horatio, clipping another of his brother's cigars as he paced the penthouse in his dressing-gown with dragons. 'Let us remember the words of our great Queen Victoria—"There is no depression in this house. We are not interested in the possibilities of defeat. They do not exist." We will, my boy, simply *reculer pour mieux sauter*. We must recapture the spirit of the dark days of the War. We must march on to victory over our troubles. Pray do not worry your young mind so much. Something is bound to turn up.'

'We can't simply go on lighting candles to St. Micawber,' returned Teddy Brickwood pretty sharply from his chair, where he'd settled down to occupy the morning with the manuscript of a thousand-page American novel about the sex life of the inhabitants of the Bronx Zoo.

'My dear lad!' Uncle Horatio looked pained. 'You do seem to be severe with me these days. It really is most unfair. You must realize that you owe your elders some respect, you know.'

Teddy said nothing. Relations with his uncle had deteriorated since their departure from the Trafalgar Club. He had immediately sent a cable to his father saying, RETURN HOME AT ONCE, to which he had the reply, REGRET NEGOTIATIONS

IN CRITICAL STAGE KEEP EVERYTHING OUT
NEWSPAPERS SUNSHINE HERE DELIGHTFUL. No
more duns had appeared, certainly, though he
noticed his uncle collected the post every
morning and took it to read in the bath. As a
week had passed, Teddy had adopted the
fatalistic view of a survivor from a severe
earthquake, wondering if there would be any
further tremors.

'I faced many more alarming crises in my time
out East,' Lord Brickwood continued, flicking
the gold-plated table-lighter he'd bought from a
pretty salesgirl that first afternoon in Bond
Street. 'My business in the Portuguese colony of
Macao—at one time, I might add, an extremely
flourishing one—was always open to
interference from trouble-makers on both sides
of the law.'

'And what exactly,' demanded Teddy,
looking up again, 'happened to be your business
in Macao, Uncle?'

'Didn't I ever tell you, dear boy? A
pardonable oversight, I feel, as I have had so
much on my mind. I operated a small
establishment where sailors and so on could
divert themselves harmlessly in the evenings.
There was fan-tan for very modest stakes. The
drinks were, I assure you, at most reasonable
prices. I even engaged one or two local young
ladies to provide a little tone in the place. I fancy
I was doing a social service, keeping those

restless young men off the streets. However, there was again jealousy in official quarters. A man of enterprise must always expect it. After a while I thought it less trouble if I closed.'

He puffed his cigar contemplatively at the window.

'Our position conceals many advantages,' he reflected. 'Our purchases of victuals and various goods were luckily made towards the beginning of the month, so the accounts will not trouble us for a week or so yet. Admittedly, we have been obliged to economize by dismissing our excellent domestic staff, and are even bereft of that peculiar Mrs. whatever her name was with the mop. But you are doing wonders, my boy, with the Hoover. I am myself, of course, totally untrained in any household duties. Really I find it an enormous relief being here alone. One can think so much more clearly when not surrounded by dozens of people.'

He flicked a speck of cigar ash off one of his dragons.

'And we were, luckily, plentifully supplied already with whisky and cigars,' he ended.

'But no food,' Teddy pointed out.

'My dear fellow, no gentleman need ever worry where his next meal is coming from. You are anyway not giving me credit for my business acumen. I noticed in your father's bookshelf an excellent little book called the *Gourmet's Guide*. With a little ingenuity we should be able to obtain the positions of the publisher's representatives—or at least, we could give that impression—and obtain two square meals a day without cost all over London. We'd get much better food and service that way too,' he added. 'You yourself, with your talent for the pen, can always make a little cash on the side by writing gossip for that morning paper there. I could supply enough tittle-tattle to keep you busy for a year, and you would have no difficulty about landing the job. Lord Chough, who owns the beastly thing, is an old crony of mine. I happen to be in possession of certain information about him and a young woman called Vi.'

'That,' announced Teddy bleakly, 'would be blackmail. The foulest of all crimes,' he added.

Lord Brickwood sighed. 'The ingenuousness of youth! Of course blackmail isn't a foul crime. You have to do something pretty nasty to be subjected to it in the first place. With all the others, you don't. Anyway I haven't heard another squeak out of Elaine Norrimer,' he remembered with this remark. 'With a bit of luck, she'll have realized my present financial position makes it hardly worth the solicitors' fees. Grace Prothero,' he added grimly, 'on the phone yesterday suggested the first of July for our nuptials. She is a lady of excellent qualities, whom I am sure would make anyone a worthy and loving wife,' he mentioned vaguely. 'But if only you, Teddy, would patch up your little squabble with the Fitzhammond girl—'

Teddy threw the manuscript aside and stood up.

'Uncle, I'm absolutely sick and tired of you, and pretty well everyone else in the family, treating me as the prospective gander to the goose who lays the golden egg. It so happens I loved Abigail once, and the thought of beastly money never came into it. She is completely uncontaminated by cash. All we wanted was a little flat where Abigail could do the cooking and we could walk in the park on Sundays and go to Aldermaston every Easter. Anyway, that's all over and done with,' he ended, giving the thousand-page novel a kick. 'Now she'd gone off with somebody else, and jolly good luck to them, I say.'

There was a silence. Teddy sat down again and glumly shuffled together the pages of the novel. Lord Brickwood stood staring at him, deep in thought for so long his cigar went out.

'Teddy,' he announced at last, in a low solemn voice, 'you are absolutely right. Yes, completely and utterly right! I have myself, alas, been steeped so long in the bitter waters of commerce to forget the springlike freshness of my own youthful outlook. I had a very moving experience this morning in the bath,' he added.

Teddy said nothing.

'In the daily paper—not *The Times*, but Lord Chough's comic one—there was a stirring article by this wonderful man, Professor Needler.'

'Needler!' Teddy scattered the manuscript all over the floor again.

His uncle opened the paper to reveal Professor Needler's crew-cut and glasses under the heading GET WITH HAPPINESS NOW SAYS TV'S PHILOSOPHER.

'While you were out last Sunday afternoon,' went on Lord Brickwood, 'I happened to fiddle idly with the telly knobs, and found myself in his presence. He had just evolved what he describes as the new prepackaged philosophy for the 'sixties. The sordidness of modern life is in our own hearts. Let us throw it out and look for the true and beautiful things about us. One phrase so sticks in my mind—"The pure springs of justice cascade eternally in their timeless caverns close below our feet." I do wish you wouldn't laugh, Teddy, I'm being utterly serious,' he added testily.

'I'm sorry, Uncle. It's just that I—well, I was acquainted with Professor Needler.'

'You were a very fortunate young man. I understand he is starting quite a movement throughout the country. Wonderful what you can do with that little box. Somehow one should be able to make money out of the idea,' he added vaguely, relighting his cigar. 'Anyway, Professor Needler has quite decided me to turn over a new leaf. I am still an active and intelligent man, bursting with original ideas. I am going to take a step I have never before ventured in my life. I am about to seek employment.'

'Quite, Uncle. What as?' asked Teddy.

Lord Brickwood made a wide gesture with his cigar. 'I may say modestly that I am a man of so many talents and such varied experience that almost anything would suit me. I have had an advertisement inserted in the Personal column this very morning.'

He handed Teddy a slip of paper from his dressing-gown pocket, which announced:

'Peer of the Realm, middle-aged, pleasing appearance and manners, many years experience administration home and abroad, seeks remunerative employment. Loyal, hard-working, co-operative, healthy, knowledgable arts and sporting activities, fluent speaker, driving licence, sense of humour, firm grasp on money.'

'The word "matters" has been omitted there after "money",' Lord Brickwood observed, reading over Teddy's shoulder. 'I really can't see how this advertisement will fail to bring a shoal of replies. I shall simply be able to pick the highest salary, and once I'm on my feet again dispense with Mrs. Prothero—that is, she would wish me to establish myself before—oh, do see who's at the door,' he broke off crossly as the bell rang.

On the mat was George Churchyard.

'What have you done with Abigail?' Teddy demanded at once.

'Abigail? I haven't done anything with Abigail,' George returned smartly. 'I'd like you to meet a friend of mine,' he went on, producing a slim girl with long blond hair and a leopard-skin two-piece. 'Morag and I are starting up in the decorating business,' he explained. 'But Abigail is exactly what I came to see you about.'

'Perhaps you will introduce me to your friends?' interrupted Lord Brickwood jovially. 'I must apologize for my *déshabillé*,' he added to Morag, indicating his dressing-gown as Teddy obliged. 'But I have, alas, not been brought up to face the serious affairs of the day quite so early in the morning.'

'The dragons look splendidly masculine,' murmured Morag.

'You think so?' said Lord Brickwood, seeming pretty pleased at this.

'To the point of barbarity, darling.'

'What's all this about Abigail, anyway?' Teddy broke in impatiently. 'I thought you'd run off with her?'

'Me? Don't be stupid.'

'I never had a damn word out of you after you'd trooped round to see Fabian—'

'I'm afraid I didn't have an awful lot of chance to put things to him,' George confessed awkwardly. 'He's terribly busy, you know, telephones and secretaries buzzing all over the place. I'll explain everything that happened. Though I think you'd better sit down first,' he added thoughtfully.

George Churchyard recited his log of the voyage of the *Snowdonia*, not forgetting Mervyn.

'I only got back to Southampton yesterday, and I've been fully occupied congratulating myself on my survival ever since,' he ended. 'And I certainly shouldn't have survived at all if Morag hadn't come down to that ghastly washing-up place with a few fags and a bottle of beer occasionally.'

'I felt *exactly* like Elizabeth Fry in those prisons, darling,' breathed Morag, inserting a cigarette into her sugar-tongs affair.

'Well . . . what do you suppose I ought to do now?' asked Teddy hopelessly, thoughts tumbling about as his brain revolved like a spin-dryer.

'My dear boy, it's perfectly simple,' Lord Brickwood cut in briskly. 'This bounder Mervyn has clearly stolen the girl's affections. You'd better charge along straight away and pinch 'em back again.'

'I—don't know if I could,' Teddy faltered.

'Oh, do wake up, Teddy!' Uncle Horatio stamped his foot. 'I keep reading in the papers the entire youth of this country are a bunch of sex-maniacs. All I can say, it's high time you joined in the fun.'

'Very well.' Teddy jumped up. He threw out his chest, nearly ruining his costal cartilages again. 'I'll go round to Berkeley Square this very minute. Except—' he hesitated, 'I don't think I've got any money for a taxi and some flowers—'

'For heaven's sake, boy! I can provide you with the necessary for that sort of thing. Or perhaps your friend here,' Uncle Horatio added, fumbling in his dressing-gown pocket. 'I have not yet had a chance to go out to the bank—'

'I'll take the bus,' declared Teddy briefly. 'Yes, right away, I'm going to—'

'One moment, my boy.' Lord Brickwood held up his hand. 'Far be it from me to temper your most natural enthusiasm at this moment, but I always believe that no gentleman ever calls on a lady before ten in the morning, whatever the circumstances. We have all had an exhausting *quart d'heure*, and a cup of coffee would not come amiss, I think? I will leave you two lads discussing the ways and means of the situation, if this charming young lady will accompany me to the kitchen and do the honours? Our staff are unfortunately taking their Easter holidays...'

'You are interested in interior decorating, I gather?' Lord Brickwood asked Morag, when they were alone in the kitchen.

'Oh, wildly,' she replied, scraping the dregs from two or three tins of instant coffee.

164

'But how charming! I think it is the decorating which makes the home, don't you?'

'Utterly, darling.'

'This flat—' Lord Brickwood stared round him critically. 'The décor is, I hasten to say, not my own taste. But you can see, with your practised eye, that is is in a sorry state of repair.'

'An absolute ruin,' agreed Morag, watching the kettle.

'It would be so nice,' suggested Lord Brickwood, 'if you could perhaps turn your attention to it? Though no doubt your fees are quite expensive—?'

'Positively exorbitant, darling.'

'But I am never one to shirk paying for the best advice available. Could you call alone some time and give me an estimate?'

'Perhaps,' concurred Morag, turning off the gas.

'One evening?' suggested Lord Brickwood, edging along the stove.

'Could be, darling.'

'You know,' he breathed heavily, 'I find you a deliciously attractive young woman.'

'And you,' murmured Morag, 'awake inside me strange, strange feelings.'

'What of?' asked Uncle Horatio, raising his eyebrows.

'Nausea,' purred Morag, picking up the tray and making for the drawing-room.

CHAPTER NINETEEN

'Hello, Abigail,' said Teddy Brickwood.

'Hello, Teddy,' said Abigail.

He found her alone in the Berkeley Square drawing-room, a whacking great place where the attentions of Morag's chums had been lavished expensively all round

'I haven't seen you for some time,' added Teddy.

'No,' agreed Abigail. 'You haven't.'

There was a silence.

'I've been away,' she explained.

'I—I hope you had nice weather?' he enquired.

'Yes,' Abigail informed him. 'Quite nice.'

Teddy wandered among the furniture for a bit.

'Abigail,' he broke out suddenly, 'you know I've been sent down from Oxford?'

She nodded. 'There was something in the papers.'

'But I'm not going to let it make any difference to my life,' he declared stoutly. 'I'm going to take a job, and work like stink and make a terrific success of it, believe you me.'

'I'm sure you will, Teddy,' asserted Abigail, making little patterns with her Rayne's toecap on the carpet.

'In no time at all I intend to be in the position of offering a girl a modest but nevertheless wholesome and loving home.'

Abigail nodded.

'Oh, Abigail!' He moved quickly on to the arm of her chair. 'I can't understand how I was so utterly idiotic and beastly to you about those stupid fish.'

'Not at all, Teddy,' she returned slowly. 'It was me who was being so horrible. Anyway, I think they were quite delightful fish, really.'

'Not that it matters a damn now,' Teddy continued decisively. 'I've had the little things put down. But Abigail—how I've missed you!'

'Oh, Teddy! And how I've missed you, too.'

'It's so wonderful just to be in the same room with you again, Abigail.'

'That's just what I feel, Teddy.'

'Abigail, surely you and I can—'

The door opened.

'This is Mr. Mervyn Spode,' Abigail announced. 'My fiancé.'

Teddy jumped up. He felt that somebody had removed all his joints and substituted plasticine instead. The room quivered and flashed about him like the telly in a thunderstorm. His mouth fell open and there was a noise in his ears like Professor Needler's pure springs of justice cascading eternally in their timeless caverns close below his feet. Finally managing to focus he observed before him a slight, pale, fair-haired figure in lavender-coloured tweeds.

'Hello, there,' Mervyn Spode greeted him. 'Didn't know you had visitors, my angel.'

'This is Teddy Brickwood,' Abigail introduced him dully. 'Mr. Brickwood,' she explained to her fiancé, 'is a very old friend. Of the family,' she added.

'Any old friend of yours, my wonderful one, is an old friend of mine,' smiled Mervyn Spode, shaking hands damply. 'How awfully good of you, Mr. Brickwood, to call so promptly to congratulate us. As a matter of fact, it's all deliciously secret at the moment. My darling bunny thought we'd better keep the press hounds at bay for just a day or two. But it'll all be in tomorrow's evening papers,' he added with satisfaction, helping himself from the cigarette box.

'I'm so glad,' Teddy managed to articulate.

'But my dear Mr. Brickwood—I can call him Teddy, surely, my darling?—you too shall be a recipient of the little silver-edged card inviting you to St. George's, Hanover Square, and afterwards at the Dorchester—Oh, Sydenham,' he broke off, throwing himself rather decoratively on the sofa as the chap in striped pants came in. 'Get me some breakfast, will you? Bacon and eggs and that sort of thing.'

'I'm afraid breakfast has already been served, sir.'

'Well, you'll have to serve some more, won't

you?' returned Mervyn with a chilly smile. 'You really can't expect me to get up at the crack of dawn for the convenience of my servants. Oh, and Sydenham—'

'Sir?'

'I'd like you to have my room changed. Terribly noisy on the front. All the traffic rushing round the corner. Taxis positively honking their way through the night.'

'I'll see what can be arranged, sir.'

'Good.' Mervyn dismissed him with a nod. 'I'm staying with my fiancée while my flat in Chelsea's being redecorated,' he continued in Teddy's direction. 'That was why I had to leave London for a couple of weeks on this cruise. And for my health, of course,' he added, giving a cough. 'But do you know, Teddy, if it hadn't been for the pure chance of my taking a voyage on that ship I should never have met Abigail?'

'No?' asked Teddy blankly.

'And we absolutely fell in love at first sight. Didn't we, my sweet?'

'Yes,' said Abigail.

It would be far more helpful, and much more conducive to the safety of ocean travel, if they displayed on the stern of ocean-going liners not that rather obvious warning KEEP CLEAR OF PROPELLERS, but instead something like DON'T SAY YES TILL YOU'RE ASHORE. Abigail had stayed late on the boat deck as the *Snowdonia* had turned finally homewards into the English

169

Channel. It was a wonderful night with the stars giving one of their Command performances, and what with the soft gurgle of the sea against the ship's side, the warm breeze blowing through her hair, and, of course, Mervyn, when the fellow raised the question of troths Abigail had plighted on the nail.

But in the twenty-four hours she had got to know Mervyn on solid ground, certain reservations had been creeping into the girl's mind. It wasn't so much that he wore built-up shoes. After all, she told herself fairly, not all men can be born six-footers. And if he ponged rather of Cologne, she supposed many males these days applied a dab or two of after-shave lotion. Mervyn's moving into Berkeley Square, she reflected, could only indicate how affectionately he wanted to be near her. And if he did boss the butler a bit, she conceded that even long-established servants need to be kept constantly up to the mark.

Abigail's main concern was her fiancé not going down all that well with the family. She was aware of this being a pretty common complication of the engaged condition, and indeed she couldn't help admiring Mervyn for the way he had overlooked certain little coolnesses in his reception. But she herself had sensed an atmosphere. Particularly when her father had drawn her aside to announce his intention of shooting on her wedding-day

170

Mervyn, her, himself, and if convenient the clergyman.

'We shall be getting married on July the thirtieth,' Mervyn continued lightly, picking a carnation from the vase beside him and sticking it into his buttonhole. 'I'm quite certain the newspapers will describe it as the wedding of the year.'

'It was always going to be,' observed Teddy flatly.

'The honeymoon, I think, my sweet,' Mervyn continued to Abigail, 'could be spent very pleasantly in your father's villa at Malaga. I don't want anything very elaborate, you know. Just a few simple weeks entirely alone in each other's company.'

'Yes,' said Abigail.

'I've been thinking about our final arrangements in London.' Mervyn continued, putting up his feet on the coffee table. 'I believe I heard somewhere your father has the lease of a house in Knightsbridge? That would suit me excellently. Near the West End, and plenty of room for entertaining all my friends. My work, of course, depends enormously on contacts— Must you go?' he added, noticing Teddy rising.

'I have an old relative waiting at home,' Teddy muttered.

'Do call. Any time.'

'Yes, I—I will. Good-bye, Abigail.'

'Good-bye, Teddy.'

They shook hands, staring into each other's eyes.

'I expect you know your way out?' mentioned Mervyn uneasily, when this had been going on for the best part of five minutes.

'Eh? Oh, yes. Good morning.'

Teddy strode through the door without a glance. He strode heavily down the stairs. He was striding across the hall when the front door opened and Fabian Fitzhammond hurried in.

'Teddy!' he gasped. 'Thank God! You've shot him?'

'Oh, hello,' Teddy greeted Fabian dully.

'Or at least you've done him grievous bodily harm, preferably where it hurts most? That ghastly wart Spode.'

Teddy shrugged his shoulders. 'If he's the one Abigail wants,' he announced, 'then I can only wish the pair of them every happiness.'

'But, dammit, the girl must have been mad! Mad! That reminds me'—he picked up a telephone. 'Do you know the man's an undischarged bankrupt?' he went on to Teddy, dialling a number. 'Antiques in the King's Road. A pretty shady business at the best of times, I'd say. Father's been checking up on him, and is he furious! He's sacked half the shipping staff and fused all the electronic computers. That toad Spode's got the lot—unpaid bills, moonlight flits, pretty near false pretences now and then. God knows how he's avoided the nick. And that's not to mention women—Hello? Mr. Fabian here. Can I speak to my secretary? That you Janet? Got that information yet? Umm... Yes... The *Quantock*, you say? How old is the ship? Prewar? Good. Just out of mothballs? Excellent. Where's she bound? Persian Gulf to New Guinea run. That's where the head-hunters are. How long away from the U.K.? Two years at a time. Fine. Sailing tonight? Immediate memo to the Marine Superintendent, and Captain Kettlehorn is to assume command.'

'If Abigail loves Mervyn—' started Teddy, as Fabian Fitzhammond put down the telephone.

'Love him? I bet she's about as much in love with him as she is with Sydenham.'

'But if she doesn't really like him,' conceded Teddy thoughtfully, 'then surely you could call the whole thing off pretty easily? I mean, she and I didn't have the slightest trouble.'

Fabian gave a hard laugh. 'Not that baby. You couldn't winkle him out with a squad of Commandos and flame-throwers. Couldn't the pair of you elope, or something? We'd make it terribly easy. Sydenham would hold the ladder and you could borrow my Maserati. Where the devil are you taking all that to?' he demanded, as Sydenham himself appeared with a tray.

'To Mr. Spode in the drawing-room, sir. It's his breakfast.'

'Breakfast? Breakfast? At this time of the day?'

'Mr. Spode ordered it specially, sir.'

'Oh, did he?' Fabian grabbed the tray. 'I think I'll serve Mr. Spode with his breakfast myself, Sydenham. I shall have great pleasure in telling him exactly what he can do with it.'

CHAPTER TWENTY

'My dear Teddy!' announced Lord Brickwood, when his nephew got back to Eaton Square. 'I should like you to meet a couple of new friends of mine.'

His uncle was now fully dressed, and had installed in the penthouse drawing-room a little fat man in a brown suit and a little fatter woman in a mink cape and a hat with pink roses round it. Teddy eyed them without enthusiasm. Apart from anything else, he had been doing some pretty heavy thinking en route and wanted an urgent talk with Uncle Horatio alone.

'Mr. and Mrs. Bliss,' Lord Brickwood went on. 'From Bacup.'

'How do you do,' nodded Teddy politely, as Uncle Horatio handed Mr. Bliss the cigar box.

'I must apologize that I cannot offer you refreshment appropriate to the hour of the morning,' Lord Brickwood went on to his guests. 'I fear we a little disorganized in our

174

domestic arrangements since our excellent butler was called away by the illness of his aged parents. Poor fellow, I could hardly refuse him. He is an only child.'

Mrs. Bliss drew up her shoulders and pursed her lips. She seemed moved to comment on the situation.

'Blood is thicker than water, I always say,' she observed.

'Exactly,' agreed Lord Brickwood. 'Mr. and Mrs. Bliss have called in response to my advertisement,' he explained to Teddy. 'You will allow me to speak freely before my young nephew here? He acts as my confidential secretary. Mr. and Mrs. Bliss,' he went on, lighting his caller's cigar for him, 'have during the past winter enjoyed a certain good fortune. Through the application of skill and knowledge acquired with many pains over the years, Mr. Bliss has at last received monetary recognition of his perseverance. Mr. Bliss,' continued Uncle Horatio, puffing his own cigar, 'has, I am glad to say, received a bounty from those excellent institutions which keep alight the spirit of hope in homes both great and humble throughout the land. I refer, of course, to the football pools. Two hundred thousand pounds—'

'Two hundred and forty thousand,' admitted Mr. Bliss, shifting awkwardly on the sofa.

'I for one would not begrudge you a penny of it,' said Lord Brickwood frankly. 'I regard these football pools as exactly what the country needs for the redistribution of incomes. So much more fun than socialism. You will find me one of the most democratic of men, I assure you. As I always maintain, the pure springs of justice cascade eternally in their timeless caverns close below our feet.'

'My Lord—' began Mr. Bliss.

'Do call me Horatio. Edgar and Sal, isn't it?'

'O' course, we're quite ordinary people, Horatio. Not that we were ever poverty-stricken, by a long chalk. In Bacup I was pretty well known in the building line.'

'The building line?' Lord Brickwood's face, already aglow, lit up further. 'I have in my time performed many fascinating deals in real estate,' he reflected. 'I have a large project on hand out East this very moment. Later you might like to have a chat about it, purely from interest.'

'I put a cross in the "No Publicity" panel on the coupon,' Edgar explained. 'Sal and I decided to keep it a secret in Bacup until we'd sorted ourselves out, like. Mind you, it was a pity missing going on the telly and that.'

'An admirable exercise in self-restraint.'

'And the man from the pools warned us about being prey to unscrupulous people.'

Sal bunched herself up again. 'A fool and his money are soon parted, I always say,' she declared.

'We didn't want to make a spectacle of

176

ourselves when we started mixing with the moneyed classes,' Edgar explained. 'We wanted someone to give us the lowdown on the social graces, like. To introduce us to the right sort of folks. That's why we've travelled down to London.'

'And you have come to exactly the right person,' Lord Brickwood assured them handsomely. 'What on earth is it, Teddy? Surely you know better than to stand making such noises in company?'

'Uncle, I've got to speak to you,' insisted Teddy, who had been hopping from foot to foot for some minutes trying to edge into the conversation. 'Alone.'

'Really, my boy!' Uncle Horatio inspected him loftily through his monocle. 'Can't you see it would be extremely bad manners to leave our charming guests to their own devices? You can place yourselves in my hands with the greatest confidence,' he continued to the Blisses. 'I suggest that for a start we take luncheon today with my very old friend the Earl of Thanet.'

'The Earl of Thanet?' exclaimed the couple, sitting up. 'You mean you know him, personal like?' asked Edgar.

'I most certainly do know him personal like,' beamed Uncle Horatio. 'Tom Thanet and I were very close indeed in the days of our youth. Many a happy weekend have I spent enjoying his liberal hospitality at Cheevers. Though of

177

course almost the entire country,' he chuckled, 'knows old Tom these days.'

The Earl of Thanet is one of those chummy earls, who throw wide the country seat and keep appearing on the telly and judging dog shows and beauty contests.

'You have a car, Edgar? Excellent. My Rolls is being serviced at the moment. We can easily reach Cheevers in time for luncheon. No doubt Tom will wish to show you round his pictures— he has large numbers of van Dycks, van Goghs, Cézannes, Constables, Goyas, El Grecos, and so on—and to point out some of his more interesting treasures. I remember to this day a suit of armour one of his ancestors wore at the Battle of Blenheim. Teddy, *do* stop making those noises, I implore you.'

'You're sure it's going to be all right, like—?' asked Edgar doubtfully.

'I need only get Tom on the telephone, and I know he will be delighted. You will find him a very nice person indeed.'

'Kind hearts—' began Sal.

'Are more than coronets,' supplied Lord Brickwood. 'How entirely right you are. Teddy, I shall really have to ask you to leave the room—'

'Uncle Horatio—' Teddy eyed him. 'I must speak to you alone this minute. I have some news about the Trafalgar Club.'

Lord Brickwood's monocle dropped out.

178

'Oh, very well, very well,' he agreed hastily. 'I used to be a member there,' he explained. 'If you would excuse us for one second . . . Now what the hell is it?' he demanded, when the pair of them were alone in the dining-room next door.

'It isn't about the Trafalgar Club, really,' Teddy confessed at once.

'Then why the devil did you give me a nasty turn like that, you young cur? Don't you know what a shocking state my nerves are in these days?'

'It's about Abigail.'

In the bus from Berkeley Square Teddy had made a painful decision. Uncle Horatio, he felt, though admittedly having his faults, was just the one to cook up a scheme for ridding Abigail of the ghastly pale-faced, wispy-haired, simpering, lavender-suited, scented, sword of Damocles hanging so precariously over her.

'You see, Abigail—' he started.

'Abigail? Haven't you made it up with the girl?' asked his uncle testily.

'I want your advice—'

'My dear boy, I have already loaded you like a packhorse with my advice about Abigail. You really can't expect me to turn my mind to such problems now.'

'But Uncle,' said Teddy in disappointment. 'A simply frightful crisis has developed, and you're the only one—'

'Other and brighter stars have risen over our horizons,' Lord Brickwood interrupted more genially. 'Admittedly, the Blisses are not exactly my idea of boon companions, and they come from this peculiar place which sounds like a digestive disorder—'

'Uncle,' cut in Teddy sternly, 'you are not to do anything in the slightest underhand.'

'Underhand?' Uncle Horatio looked shocked. 'It distresses me to say so, Teddy, but you are becoming quite a little prig. Anyway, the only other replies to the advertisement were a couple of moneylenders and some people wanting me to sell encyclopaedias at the door. Me! At the door! Encyclopaedias! Really!'

'So you're really going to impose those people on your pal the Earl of Thanet?'

'I don't know him from Adam, of course,' Lord Brickwood admitted easily, picking up a brochure from the dining-table. 'But that peculiar pair will be perfectly happy if they think I do. With a little ingenuity at Cheevers I should be able to buy tickets on the quiet, and after announcing that some mistake has been made stand luncheon in the cafeteria—the menu, I understand, is quite excellent of its sort. It says in the brochure that the Earl appears during the afternoon to chat with his visitors—after all, the public can always stare at pictures in the National Gallery, but to gorp at an Earl is a bit of a treat—when I shall quite easily be able to suggest that he and I are on terms of great intimacy. I am sure the outing will be a valuable demonstration of my bona fides. We must remember to keep half the tickets,' Lord Brickwood added, inspecting the brochure through his monocle. 'They allow you to get reduced admission at Woburn.'

'Uncle,' declared Teddy firmly, 'you're mad.'

'Young man, you will shortly force me to read you a lecture on disrespect. We must not neglect our guests any longer,' Lord Brickwood added, making for the drawing-room door. 'They are somewhat shy, and might easily slip off behind our backs. My apologies, my apologies,' he announced to the Blisses. 'I took the opportunity of telephoning Tom at the same time. You will enjoy Cheevers, situated as it is on the edge of the glorious North Downs within easy reach of London, with magnificent views and every amenity for the visitor. Afterwards...' He made a wide gesture with his cigar. 'The whole London season lies before us as delightfully as a dozen unopened oysters. Ascot, Henley, Eton and Harrow at Lord's, the Royal Academy, Glyndebourne, Cowes, Swan Upping.... We shall do the lot. Together.'

'About your fees, my Lord—Horatio, that is,' mumbled Edgar, as Teddy shifted from foot to foot again. 'If you could favour me with an estimate—'

Lord Brickwood held up a hand. 'We can go

181

into that at a later stage. No gentleman, I believe, ever discusses money before luncheon.'

'You know you can rely on me to see you right.'

'I am sure I can rely upon you to see me more than right,' beamed Lord Brickwood. 'Ever been to Buckingham Palace?' he added mysteriously. 'Now I think we should be on our way—oh, do answer the door, Teddy. Explain I am definitely not at home.'

'Oh, all right,' he agreed shortly.

Outside was the woman from the steps of the Trafalgar Club, still with the dead animal round her neck.

'Lord Brickwood is definitely not at home,' she began at once, with a nice smile.

'I'm afraid that he really—'

'Dear old Waffles! His voice always did carry so. It kept getting him into terrible trouble with hotel managements. I'd like to see him, please.'

'As a matter of fact, he's just on the point of going out,' added Teddy quickly.

'All the more reason I should see him now,' she continued, with another nice smile. 'Because it will be very unlikely that he will ever come back again.'

'If you like, I'll tell him you're here,' Teddy faltered.

'Please do,' she smiled again. 'If he's not very enthusiastic, just mention King's Lynn.'

'Uncle, there's a Miss Norrimer called,' he

182

announced in the drawing-room. 'About King's Lynn.'

'King's Lynn!' Lord Brickwood's monocle fell out again. The colour of his cheeks turned from smoked salmon to frozen cod. 'Good God ... I ... A lady who is doing some typing for me,' he explained to the Blisses. 'I am preparing a book, you know, about various British resorts. The Government have rather pushed me into it. The King's Lynn section is an extremely difficult one, and if you would permit me a few moments alone with her to correct it before leaving for Cheevers...? Most understanding of you,' he added, as the Blisses rose smartly. 'The printers are waiting, as usual. Teddy, please show our guests into the dining-room. And for God's sake come back,' he muttered. 'I'm not saying anything without a witness.'

'A charming man, that Lord Brickwood,' remarked Edgar, as Teddy bustled them through.

'He has a certain way with him,' Teddy nodded.

'I'm rather hoping,' Edgar whispered to Teddy with a glance at his wife's back, 'he'll show me a bit of life, like.'

'I'm quite sure he'll show you a bit of life like,' Teddy agreed, shutting the door.

'My dear Elaine, you haven't changed a scrap,' Lord Brickwood greeted his new guest. 'What part are you playing at the moment?'

'Landlady of a Kensington boarding-house,' she replied sweetly. 'As I have for the past ten years.'

'You've left the stage?' He shook his head sadly. 'Dear me, what a loss! Terribly glad you bothered to look in for a few moments. One so loses track of one's old friends.'

'As a matter of fact, I may not have to detain you very long.' Elaine Norrimer sat down and threw her dead animal over the arm of the chair. 'You can get rid of me in a couple of minutes, Waffles, simply by writing a cheque for ten thousand pounds.'

Lord Brickwood's monocle fell out again.

'But my dear Elaine! We are not back in the 'thirties, you know, when income tax was so modest you didn't even bother to fiddle it.'

'Your letters and other documents,' she went on, patting her handbag, 'would cheer up those awful little income tax men no end. I could imagine them all getting so excited as they opened them on a Monday morning. I expect they have terribly dreary lives, really. And so do the ones who toil away with all those beastly piles of documents done up with red tape for the Director of Public Prosecutions—'

'Elaine! This is all as much in the past as cloche hats and Ivor Novello—'

'The law has a long arm, Waffles,' observed Elaine pleasantly, giving her animal a stroke. 'No doubt it has a long memory as well. As it

184

happens, ten thousand would come in terribly handy just now for the renovations. You can't imagine the cost of keeping a boarding-house habitable for yourself, let alone the residents. There's rewiring, for a start. An amazingly costly activity, rewiring. The plumbing, of course—'

'Elaine, I just haven't got ten thousand.'

'Indeed? My spies say you have been living like Crœsus on an expense account ever since you came home.'

'Elaine, you wouldn't do this to me,' Lord Brickwood tried again.

'I would, you know. After all, I feel you owe me a little something for all those years we spent together. Ascot, Torquay, Worthing, Bath, Ilfracombe if I remember, Poole—'

'Elaine—' Lord Brickwood stared at the carpet. 'Elaine, I have something very, very serious to say to you. Teddy, please go into the kitchen. You may come back in five minutes. You might see if there's anything to eat overlooked in some corner or other while you're about it.'

Teddy sat on the kitchen table, biting his lip. The doubt he had cast on his uncle's sanity had been no idle remark. He began to fear that long residence in the tropical sun had deranged the old boy's brain, which wasn't to mention the strain of all those problems he seemed to pile on it. He wondered if his father's doctor might be persuaded to come round and have the chap tidied away into some institution for a bit. Far from invoking Uncle Horatio to free Abigail from the pallid understudy who had taken over his own part in her life, he realized he wouldn't have a chance to try himself once uncle was let loose on the London season with two hundred and forty thousand quid. But he hadn't got far with all this before the kitchen door opened and Uncle Horatio announced:

'Teddy! My boy! You must be the very first to hear. I have some absolutely wonderful news for you. Elaine and myself have just become engaged to be married.'

'What!' He fell off the table.

'Come, my boy.'

Teddy followed his uncle back to the sitting-room.

'The workings of Fate,' announced Lord Brickwood, clasping Elaine's hand as it rested on the dead animal, 'are inscrutable. Elaine and I were friends—very close friends—in those gay days when Hyperion won the Derby, the sun shone everywhere in the British Empire, and fags were a bob for twenty. In those times, Teddy, I was young. A lad hardly older than yourself. I was too bashful ever to bring myself to the point of proposing marriage to the lady I adored and revered. But Fate,' he explained, exchanging smiles with Elaine, 'has brought us together in our riper, maturer years. How much more delightful, now our youthful frivolities are well behind us, that we should spend the afternoon of our lives together. Kismet—'

'But what about Mrs. Prothero?' Teddy burst out.

'Mrs. Prothero? The lady I have just engaged as my housekeeper here,' he explained to Elaine. 'I'm afraid I shall have to discharge her. I am not particularly sorry. I did not feel in my heart she was ideally suited for the job.'

'Uncle—!' exclaimed Teddy.

'You'll be such a useful man about a boarding-house, Waffles dear,' murmured Elaine.

'Boarding-house? I assure you, my love, that I shall see we are installed in some far more appropriate habitation. Not of course that I'm saying your own establishment isn't on a par with the Savoy. It is not deep carpets and bowing waiters which ease the traveller's way. Not a bit. It is the feeling of being in his own home, which I am sure you, Elaine, supply so wonderfully. Teddy, take the future Lady Brickwood's bag into the lobby—'

'I think I'll keep it with me, Waffles,' smile Elaine, grabbing it.

'As you wish, as you wish,' agreed Uncle Horatio loftily. 'I was only thinking of your comfort—Damn that doorbell! Teddy, do go and get rid of them, whoever they are. This is definitely a moment when Elaine and I do not wish to be disturbed.'

Teddy came back to the room a moment later.

'Mrs. Prothero,' he announced.

CHAPTER TWENTY-ONE

'My dear, dear Gracie,' exclaimed Lord Brickwood, tripping across the drawing-room carpet as he showed her in. 'How wonderful to see you. But what a surprise!'

'As soon as I put down the telephone last night,' cooed Mrs. Prothero, 'I said to myself. Why, what a silly I am sitting here in Edinburgh while dear Horatio is all alone there in London. Why on earth, I asked myself, should we get married up in Edinburgh, anyway? We can get married just as easily in London, and I expect rather sooner because of the convenience of everything. So here I am, Horatio.'

'And there you are, Gracie,' agreed Lord Brickwood, having a quick pat at the diamonds. 'And how utterly delightful. You know my young nephew, of course,' he added, as Teddy reappeared from the direction of the kitchen. 'I'm afraid he had to go outside because he was suddenly taken a little ill. Something he ate, no doubt. Better now?' asked Lord Brickwood, raising his eyebrows urgently.

Teddy nodded. As a matter of fact, the poor

chap really was feeling pretty sick after the interesting minute or so they'd just passed.

'Mrs Prothero?' Uncle Horatio had asked, just as soon as he'd put his monocle back again. 'What on earth does she want just now? Something connected with her insurance cards, no doubt. Elaine my dear—' He turned graciously to his latest fiancée. 'I hesitate to interrupt such a tender moment, but if I don't get rid of this Prothero woman at once she'll be hanging about half the day. Talks, you know. The hind leg of a donkey is nothing to her. If you'd just slip one moment into a bedroom—'

'Not a bedroom,' returned Elaine firmly. 'Definitely not a bedroom, Waffles.'

'As you wish, my dear. Teddy, please show Elaine into the dining-room. What's that you said? I do wish you would try and control these rather disgusting noises—'

'I was saying "Bacup",' Teddy managed to get out.

'Bacup? Bacup? Oh, my God. Yes, of course. Move Bacup into a bedroom first. Bacup,' he explained to Elaine, 'is my dog. I have just acquired him—Irish wolfhound—and he is inclined to be a little savage with strangers. Our porter here was taken to hospital this very morning. I should naturally hate any harm to come to you, my dear, on this wonderful day.'

'Naturally,' smiled Elaine.

'I wonder if you'd mind frightfully shifting

for a moment into one of the bedrooms?' Teddy announced awkwardly, coming into the dining-room to find the Blisses staring at each other across the table. 'Lord Brickwood has unexpectedly got a couple of rather difficult business interviews on his hands, and he'd like to keep the parties separate.'

Edgar's eyebrows went up. 'I don't know that I'm used to being requested to queue up in a bedroom back home.'

'Quite common in London, I assure you. Terrible shortage of office accommodation.'

'If I asked my customers to discuss their foundations in *my* bedroom I'd be thought proper daft, that's straight.'

'When in Rome do as the Romans do,' Sal pointed out sharply.

'Oh, all right,' Edgar agreed, rising. 'I suppose there's worse places in the house to wait.'

'Bacup has been moved?' asked Uncle Horatio, as Teddy reappeared. 'Excellent! He was no trouble? I thought not. I fancy we will soon have him obedient. Now show Elaine into the dining-room, and as soon as you've shut the door I can admit Mrs. Prothero.'

'I am sorry, my dear Gracie, that I am unable to offer you any refreshment just at the moment,' Lord Brickwood now went on, easing his first fiancée into the chair just vacated by the later version. 'But I was just on the point of slipping out to Cheevers for luncheon. The Earl of Thanet, you know. A dear friend of mine. You shall meet him very soon.'

'How wonderful, Horatio! But now I can go down to Cheevers with you. I've always longed to meet the Earl. He has such a charming manner on television.'

'Yes, and so you can,' returned Uncle Horatio, his face dropping rather. 'Though there may be some difficulty about an extra place. I believe we are a dozen already, and of course everyone knows Tom Thanet to be shockingly superstitious. But we have many things to discuss, Gracie my dear, and there is time before we need start for Cheevers anyway. It is only fifty-five minutes by road from central London. Let us—Teddy, the door!' he commanded, as the bell rang again. 'Whoever it is—even the Duke himself—he is to be kept on the mat.'

'Thank heavens for that,' grunted Teddy, finding outside George Churchyard and Morag again.

'I say, are you all right?' asked George. 'You look rather pale.'

'Postively corpse-ish,' agreed Morag.

'I've had rather a busy morning since you left,' he managed to say. 'My uncle, you know. He's been entertaining.'

'Odd hour to entertain,' remarked George.

'Odd uncle, darling,' purred Morag.

'Anyway, can't we come in? I've got something vitally important to tell you.'

'Couldn't you possibly come back a little later?'

George shook his head. 'I've absolutely got to have a decision by one o'clock. I'm meeting him for lunch.'

'Meeting who for lunch?'

'Professor Needler.'

'Professor Needler?'

George nodded. 'Yes, didn't I tell you?'

Teddy shrugged his shoulders. 'I think we might be able to have a word in my bedroom. Please don't take any notice of anyone on the way through.'

'As I have reflected so often in my life,' Lord Brickwood was intoning as the three of them entered the drawing-room, 'the pure springs of justice cascade eternally in their timeless caverns close below our feet. I feel, Gracie, that is—'

'Friends of mine,' muttered Teddy to his uncle as they strode through. 'Dropped in for a chat.'

'Hello, darling,' murmured Morag in Lord Brickwood's direction. 'Seen any good decorations recently?'

'Sorry to disturb you,' Teddy said to Elaine, who was reading the *New Statesman* in the dining-room.

'If you *have* turned this into the waiting-room,' she remarked sweetly as the trio hurried past, 'I do wish you'd provide a few magazines with pictures in them.'

'Won't keep you a moment,' Teddy threw out to the Blisses, putting his head in his uncle's bedroom.

'Just one minute—' Edgar rose from the laundry basket. 'No discourtesy intended, mind, but I'd like an explantion of exactly what's going on here.'

'Going on? Why, absolutely nothing, Mr. Bliss. Lord Brickwood is conducting a normal morning's business, that's all.'

'Normal! I'll tell you straight, it wouldn't be called normal in Bacup.'

'No?'

'You mean it goes on like this every day?'

'Except on Sundays,' nodded Teddy.

'Many hands—' began Sal.

'Lord Brickwood won't keep you more than a moment, I'm sure,' Teddy interrupted quickly. 'I think we'll be undisturbed in here,' he continued to George and Morag, hustling them into his own bedroom next door. 'Sorry the bed's unmade and it's a bit of a mess,' he ended, 'but quite frankly, Uncle and I haven't got enough between us to buy a square meal, let alone pay someone to wash it up.'

'Then you'll be pretty pleased at my news,' George remarked, sitting on the foot of the bed. 'Just one thing first, though. This very morning Morag and I have decided to get married.'

'Really? I say, I'm jolly pleased—'

'Frightfully bourgeois, but *so* delightful,' murmured Morag, quivering a bit beneath her leopard-skin.

'We didn't want to say anything until there looked the chance of getting a foothold in life, which I'm glad to say Professor Needler of all people has provided.'

'But how on earth Professor Needler?' frowned Teddy.

'You know he's turning out some terrible tosh on the telly, a new philosophy based on all things bright and beautiful?' asked George, while Morag touched up her black eyes in the mirror. 'The public's fallen for it flat, just like they did for canasta. That satirical stuff is terribly old hat now. The British public never really likes cleverness on the stage, you know. Except in animals, of course,' he added. 'People only watched it from social conscience, anyway, like they used to give alms to the poor. Believe me, the bright and beautiful stuff is definitely *in*. I just got wind that Needler was starting a new philosophical night-club, so I rang him at the telly studios just now and asked for a job.'

'You actually rang Needler?' asked Teddy wonderingly.

'You bet I did. Apparently there's been a terrible stink at Oxford about our being chucked out. The Regius Professor himself made no end of a fuss. He's dead jealous of

Needler, of course, because he's on the other channel with his show *Greek Meets Greek*. Needler simply fell over backwards to make amends—I suppose it would hit his rating for six if we spilt the full beans to the papers. So Morag will do the décor, I'll be one of the stars, and you can write the scripts, if that's how you'd like it. What do you say?'

'Say! Good lord, George, I'd absolutely jump at any sort of night-club—satirical, philosophical, evangelical, whatever you like to name.'

'You've never made a better move,' agreed George warmly. 'I believe I can recognize a band-wagon when I hear one.'

'And Professor Needler,' threw in Morag huskily, 'has got it going with his foot flat down in overdrive.'

'One moment,' Teddy broke off. 'The door bell.'

The Blisses were still staring at each other in his uncle's bedroom. Elaine Norrimer was still reading the *New Statesman*. Lord Brickwood was still holding forth to Gracie in the drawing-room. Teddy strode silently into the hall and threw open the front door.

Outside was Mr. McInch and a pretty young Chinese girl in a cheongsam.

'Ha ha!' cried Mr. McInch.'

'Oh, hello,' said Teddy.

'Wherrre is he?' whirred Mr. McInch.

'I really don't know who—'

'Yer uncle, young man. I demand to see him at once. I hae something of the utmost importance to say to him.'

'Well, you can't see him now,' returned Teddy shortly. 'He's talking about personal matters to Mrs. Prothero.'

'Mrs. Prothero?' Mr. McInch's scrubbing-brush hair bristled a bit more. 'She's here? Och, don't stand there! I pray that I am in time.'

Giving Teddy a shove in the epigastrium with his elbow, Mr. McInch grabbed the Chinese girl by the hand and burst into the drawing-room.

'Mr. McInch!' Mrs. Prothero let out a scream and jumped up. 'What on earth are you doing in London?'

'Mrs. Prothero, I hae come to save you, body, soul, and cheque book.'

'Really, Mr. McInch! I cannot understand your pursuing me all the way from Edinburgh like this. Particularly arriving with that . . . that . . . who on earth do you have there, anyway, Mr. McInch?'

'Mrs. Prothero.' The attorney drew himself up. 'It gives me great pleasure to introduce to you Lady Brickwood.'

'Lady Brickwood!'

'Lady Brickwood,' confirmed Mr. McInch.

'Oh, hello, Lotus Seed,' murmured Lord Brickwood absently in the background.

'What on earth is the meaning of this?'

demanded Mrs. Prothero, turning a gaze like hydrochloric acid on Lord Brickwood.

He shrugged his shoulders.

'I caused enquiries to be made,' Mr. McInch went on triumphantly. 'Our agents in Hong Kong discovered that this lady, whom I had flown over at my own expense—my own expense, Mrs. Prothero—was in fact married to Lord Brickwood in Macao a year or two ago.'

'Horatio!' thundered Mrs. Prothero. 'How on earth did this happen?'

'East is East, and West is West,' was all Lord Brickwood seemed able to say. 'I suppose one rather overlooks the twain meet rather much these days.'

'What *is* happening? A fire or something?' demanded Elaine Norrimer, appearing from the dining-room. 'Really, Waffles, I've read half-way through the *New Statesman*, which is quite enough for this hour of the morning. Perhaps you'll introduce your friends?' she added.

'And this, I suppose,' cried Mrs. Prothero, 'is your other wife?'

'No,' Lord Brickwood told her, 'only my other fiancée.'

'Mr. McInch! Angus!'

'Mrs. Prothero—?'

'Get me away—away at once.'

'Don't you worry, Mrs. Prothero. Ye are in good hands again now. Your interests shall be fully protected, Mrs. Prothero—'

'Oh, Angus! Angus!' She fell into his arms, making the poor chap stagger a bit. 'Why didn't I listen to you in the first place? I was a fool, a fool!'

'Don't fret yeself, Mrs. Prothero—'

'Call me Gracie,' said Mrs. Prothero, producing a handkerchief from somewhere in the Edwardian sofa. 'Like you used to.'

'I shall look after you, Gracie. Not only as a client, but—air—wheel—if you want me to repeat that certain question I put last month as we sat alone in my office—'

'Oh, Angus!' Mrs. Prothero shoved the sofa a bit closer. 'Yes, of course. I should have accepted you there and then. You can have it in writing, if you like,' she added.

'That won't be necessary. Good morning to you all,' Mr. McInch added briskly, leading her out.

'Who the devil are you?' demanded a little fat man in a ginger tweed suit and gold-rimmed glasses just coming through the front door.

'I wouldn't say any more visitors are welcome,' replied Mr. McInch briefly.

'Visitors? It's my flat, damn it. Get out, before I call the porter. Oh, hello, Waffles,' Mr. Algernon Brickwood went on, coming into the drawing-room and dropping his briefcase. 'Having a party, I see, as usual. You never change do you? Where's Teddy? Ah, there you are, my boy. I'm glad to say the negotiations were completed under the mellowing influence of the Bahamas moon and rum punch. For twenty-four hours the old-established firm of Brickwood and Vole had been sheltering under the gold-handled umbrella of Scrutchings Books, Inc., of Madison Avenue. Although I never use my prefix of "The Honourable" here,' he reflected, 'I was delighted to find it had a solid cash value in the export market. I shall be appointed managing director in London, at a salary commensurate with my experience. Plus luncheon vouchers, of course. I foresee—'

'Teddy!'

Abigail appeared in the doorway.

'Teddy! My darling! It's all right.'

'All right?' He looked blank. For one thing it was a bit difficult to see her, what with all those people.

'That dreadful man Mervyn Spode. Fabian's bought him off. Ten thousand pounds. That was all he wanted to get engaged to me for at all.'

'Abigail! my angel!'

'Teddy, my darling!'

They met in the middle of the drawing-room, scattering the ranks. Teddy fell on her. He kissed her. Then an idea struck him. He started chewing her hair. He got through great mouthfuls of it, then thought he'd have a taste or two round the base of her neck before taking his next course off her left ear.

'Oh, Teddy, you're so wonderful,' sighed Abigail. 'As soon as I saw you again, I knew that only you could be my husband.'

Teddy tried to say something in reply, but with all that hair in your mouth it's difficult to speak clearly.

'If you'll come up for breath a minute,' demanded George Churchyard, pushing his way past, 'Morag and I can get out to land those jobs with Professor Needler.'

'Abigail and I will come too,' Teddy decided, grabbing her hand. 'See you this afternoon, Father. I'm sure Uncle Horatio has lots and lots to talk to you about first.'

The flat suddenly seemed rather empty. The four survivors stood looking at each other. The door from the kitchen slowly opened. A little fat man and a little fat woman crept nervously across the carpet towards the front door.

'Where the devil do you think you're going?' demanded Mr. Algernon Brickwood.

'Back to Bacup,' said the couple, shooting out.

'Waffles, you do seem to ask some peculiar people to your parties these days,' complained his brother. 'You haven't a quid or so on you I suppose? I want to pay off my taxi, and I've only got dollars. No? I'll scrounge off the porter. Do ask the two ladies to make themselves at home, if you wish.'

'You see, I really haven't any money,'

200

explained Lord Brickwood brokenly to Elaine. 'Not a sou. Also you observe Lotus Seed, of whom I am extremely and most genuinely fond—'

'Of course, Waffles.' She gave him another smile. 'I knew you were stony. I was just having you on. After all, you did give me the run around a teeny, teeny bit in the gay days, didn't you?'

He nodded.

'As for those letters and so on, Elaine—'

'I burnt them. The night of the first Derby after you went out East. And one thing more, Waffles—you're just as sweet now as you ever were, but I'd never marry you then and I certainly wouldn't have done now. Goodbye, Waffles. You know where to come if you both want board and lodging.'

'That's awfully good of you, Elaine—'

'Our tariff is very moderate. 'Bye.'

'Darling,' said Lady Brickwood, as they were alone. 'I so want you to come home to Hong Kong.'

Uncle Horatio nodded slowly. 'And so do I, my dear, so do I. I think we can manage to raise the fare somehow. I tried to write to you about it from the Club. Life in London is too confusing for me today. I'm like a hansom cab in the Piccadilly underpass.'

'Darling, I do so want to buy some Persil. They say in England you can wash whiter even than white.'

Uncle Horatio gave another nod, and feeling deeply into his pocket produced half a crown.

'You'll find a porter downstairs, just like our little flat in Hong Kong,' he explained. 'He'll show you the way to the shops. I'd like a moment alone to collect my thoughts.'

The door shut. He wandered round the deserted flat. He looked hopefully for the whisky decanter, but it was empty. He opened the cigar box, to find Mr. Bliss had smoked the last one. He gave a sigh.

'I'm getting old,' confessed Uncle Horatio to himself. 'At last I hear the sound of distant gravediggers. After all these years the worst is happening to me—I am *losing my touch*.'

He started, as the doorbell rang.

On the mat was a pale young man with wispy hair and a lavender tweed suit.

'I'm Mervyn Spode,' announced the young man.

'Oh, yes?' said Uncle Horatio, screwing in his monocle.

'I was rather looking for Abigail, or this young fellow Brickwood. I gathered she'd come round here.'

'But do step inside,' invited Uncle Horatio, the colour coming back to his cheeks. 'You are an—er, friend of the couple, Mr. Spode?'

Mervyn gave a laugh. 'I suppose that's exactly what you'd say I am.'

'I am young Teddy's uncle,' announced Lord Brickwood, showing him into the drawing-room. 'Lord Brickwood.'

'Oh, indeed?' Mervyn looked up. 'I didn't know he had aristocratic connexions.'

'I have been many years in business out East,' Uncle Horatio explained modestly. 'I am paying a flying visit to attend to my interests here. If you would like to wait for young Teddy—'

'Actually, I just wanted a brief word with Abigail,' Mervyn complained. 'In the general rush this morning she didn't hand me back my—a ring I once happened to give her.'

'I'm sure that oversight can very easily be righted. Indeed, I shall see to it myself.'

'Thank you,' nodded Mervyn. 'After all, it was rather costly.'

'I should like to offer you appropriate refreshment,' Lord Brickwood continued, offering a chair. 'But my excellent butler died recently, and I could never bring myself to engage another. Anyway, I do most of my entertaining in the Trafalgar Club.' He chuckled. 'If the walls of my private room there only had ears, I have often felt they would be covered not with tasteful wallpaper but with sheets of gold.'

'Oh, yes?' Mervyn looked up again.

'You will no doubt have heard my name in commercial circles here? In the East, of course, it is a financial password, if I may be permitted a little boast. I am at the moment engaged in a most exciting scheme in Hong Kong—holiday pagodas to let to visiting Americans. The Colony is quite thrilled about it.'

'That sounds rather a smart idea,' murmured Mervyn, shifting in his chair.

'It is, of course, disclosed in the strictest confidence.'

'Oh, of course.'

'I raised a million from Pott's Bank to finance it. That is why I am here at this minute, as a matter of fact. The rest—not a large sum, a hundred thousand or so—I feel obliged to offer to the small investor. They are a nuisance, but I believe the little man—by which I mean individual holdings up to ten thousand—should be allowed a stake in an enterprise which touches so deeply on the financial balance, the international good will, the very existence, I might say, of our great Commonwealth of Nations.'

'Oh, quite,' agreed Mervyn.

Uncle Horatio stood polishing his monocle in silence.

'Er—' said Mervyn after a while. 'You know, I fancy I have some spare money lying about at my bankers just at the moment.'

Lord Brickwood shook his head. 'Out of the question, I'm afraid. There is only one holding left, which I am reserving for some able young man prepared to be a working director with me out in Hong Kong. I am still searching—'

'I know a good bit about the building business,' Mervyn interrupted. 'And I've been thought pretty smart in my time. Also, for various reasons I'd like to be out of the country just now. The further out the better,' he added. 'If you think you might consider me, Lord Brickwood—?'

Uncle Horatio looked doubtful. 'We are in a hard world, Mr. Spode. I fear—and I am sure as an astute businessman yourself you will appreciate my point—I should have to see some evidence of your financial position first.'

'I happen to have a cheque for ten thousand on me,' smiled Mervyn Spode, producing it.

'In that case,' conceded Lord Brickwood, 'I think we can both congratulate ourselves on a most valuable few minutes' work. Yes, Mr. Spode, I welcome you to the Brickwood Organization.' He reached for his hat and stick. 'At the earliest possible moment you and I—and of course Lady Brickwood, I never travel without my delightful Chinese wife—shall take plane for Hong Kong, where you will be amazed at the riches of the East still awaiting the harvest of a first-class financial brain. It is just one o'clock, Mr. Spode,' went on Uncle Horatio, opening the penthouse door. 'I shall leave word for Lady Brickwood, who is out indulging in an orgy of London shopping, and you and I shall have a little luncheon together to celebrate our association. We won't go to the Trafalgar Club, but some altogether gayer restaurant. Afterwards we will step down to Old Bailey to see my solicitors—Duff and Trimm, no doubt you've heard of them? Very able firm—who will prepare the necessary documents and all can be signed, sealed, and delivered by tonight. You haven't forgotten your cheque? Excellent. You can endorse it to my business account at Pott's, which will save a great deal of trouble. "The gorgeous East",' continued Uncle Horatio, putting his arm round Mervyn's shoulders as they went down in the lift, '"with richest hand Showers on her kings barbaric pearl and gold." And you and I, Mr. Spode,' he ended as they reached the front door, 'can with a little perseverance be of that very monarchy. Taxi!'

Which just proves that Professor Needler was jolly well right. The pure springs of justice cascade eternally in their timeless caverns close below our feet.

Photoset, printed and bound in Great Britain by REDWOOD BURN LIMITED, Trowbridge, Wiltshire